BLACK WITCH

MOTH

A Man's Spiritual Journey to
Find His Destiny

A NOVEL BY

C. MICHAEL CURRY

Copyright © 2022 by C. Michael Curry

For information regarding permission, please write to:
info@barringerpublishing.com

Barringer Publishing, Naples, Florida
www.barringerpublishing.com

Design and layout by Linda S. Duider
Cape Coral, Florida

Photo on back cover by Matt Stamey

ISBN: 978-1-954396-3-19
Library of Congress Cataloging-in-Publication Data
Black Witch Moth / Curry

Printed in U.S.A.

For my parents, Betty and Percy.

AND IN MEMORY OF

Raúl Villarreal
A promise kept, Amigo.
Ashé

CONTENTS

Light and Shadows

"I had a dream last night, Amigo," I say softly.

"What did you dream about?" he asks.

"I was in the sacred space between the light and the shadows," I answer.

"I know that space," he says, smiling. "I'm glad you found it. The best way to find it is always in dreams."

Havana sits on the northern coast of Cuba—on the southern edge of the Florida Straits and ninety miles south and west of the island of Key West. The Gulf Stream coalesces west of the two islands in the Gulf of Mexico and travels at a speed of six knots to the east and north. The volume of water moving between Key West and Cuba is a staggering 8 billion gallons daily at a rate of about 96 million gallons per second. The Gulf Stream carries a volume of water greater than all the rivers on Earth combined.

A gyre, an extensive system of circular currents and powerful winds, generates the energy required to move this much water. There are six gyres on earth, the most powerful being the Gulf Stream. Anyone who has spent time in it will tell you that the energy flowing between Key West and Havana bends light in strange and surprising ways, casting shadows on all who try to make their way across.

Stories about life and death in the embrace of the great current abound. The light and shadows, uncaring and unforgiving, bear witness to the fates of those who have feared her and those who have loved her and had the courage, folly, or desperation to challenge her.

PROLOGUE

Baracoa ~ 1492

"... and I found a large bay ... and at the end of it to the southeast, there is a high square mountain which looks like an island ..."

— Christopher Columbus, Baracoa, Cuba, October 26, 1492

The chief or Cacique, in the Arawak language of the Taíno, was tied to the stake and told by a Franciscan friar about the God of the Christians and the Articles of Faith.

The Cacique, who had never heard of this before, was told that if he did not adopt the Christian articles of Faith, he would not go to Heaven but to Hell, where he would suffer eternal torment.

The Cacique, whose name was Hatuey, asked the Franciscan friar if all Christians went to heaven.

"Yes, they do," the friar said.

"Then I would prefer to go to hell."

— Cacique Hatuey, Baracoa, February 12, 1512

Sailing in three, frail, wooden ships, the Spaniards spotted the mountain they would call El Yunqué—the Anvil, rising above the horizon from six leagues to the northeast. In awe of its beauty, they sailed toward what they hoped was Asia's eastern shore. Having ventured west from Borikén into uncharted waters, they couldn't know the land ahead wasn't Asia, but the northern coast of an island called Coabana or Cuba.

Anxious to touch dry land after over a month at sea, the captain of the three ships, Christopher Columbus, faced a dilemma. It was late in the day, and getting closer to shore would be dangerous without sunlight to gauge the water's depth. Opting for caution, he ordered the ships to anchor in the deeper waters outside the entrance to a small inlet.

Once moored, Columbus stood on the port side of the *Santa Maria*, studying what appeared to be a village marked by small fires placed at intervals along the shore. The forest in the background was impenetrable in the fading light. The faint sound of drumming carried across the small bay to the anchored ships. Columbus wondered if the activity was a reaction to having spotted his small armada. It was October 1492, according to the Christian calendar.

Tíaquena, a young Taíno girl, does not know the Christian calendar. She only knows that it is a special night, the night of the full moon, the night of the ceremony. She stands on the eastern tip of the narrow beach that curves toward the mountains. To her right, she can see the entrance to the bay, where three strange objects float on the water. To her left, banana plants and coconut trees give way to a dense tropical rainforest. Thatched-roof huts line the forest's edge, forming a thin barrier between the trees and the beach. The village seems to be shrinking under the pressure of the forest and the sea. The sound of drums reaches Tíaquena, setting the tempo for the evening's event.

To the west, silhouetted against the glow of the setting sun and shrouded in a lingering mist from the afternoon rains, the flat-topped mountain the Taíno call *Yuké* or "White Earth" stands 1,900 feet above sea level. Tíaquena is thinking about the Zemi spirits living inside and the ceremony she is about to perform. From an early age, her grandmother explained that Atabey, the Zemi spirit at the center of the Taíno creation story, had chosen her to bring messages back and forth from the other side. Until today, Tíaquena thought of her grandmother's notion of her as some messenger as a distant responsibility. Now, that responsibility is about to be fulfilled.

Halfway around the bay, torches are lit, and thin trails of smoke drift into the forest on a light breeze coming off the ocean. People are gathering in the center of the village in front of Cacique's hut. The thatched covering at the entrance opens, and Cacique descends the stairs. The emergence of the chief signals the time for her to take her place.

Tíaquena spent the day fasting and meditating while the tribe's elders adorned her body with ritual shells and polished stones in preparation for the ceremony. When the women were done, she stood for a long time admiring their handiwork.

The ceremony, known as *Areyto*, is a ritual used for centuries to talk to the Zemi spirits and the tribe's ancestors. Its incantations are powerful, and its success is always uncertain. Tíaquena's grandmother told stories of how dangerous it is to be in the presence of the spirits. There were stories of those who visited never returning and more than one instance of a dancer performing the ceremony and disappearing the next day.

Apprehensive of these dangers, Tíaquena faced Yuké, took several deep breaths to settle her spirit, and prayed to her grandmother, Abéquan, who crossed to the spirit world four winters ago. Before she could remember, Abéquan had been Tíaquena's spiritual soul mate and teacher. When growing up,

Abéquan always gave her small dance steps to practice. As a result of her grandmother's patience and persistence, Tíaquena learned much of the sacred dance and many of the folk dances by the time she was six years old.

"Give me the strength, Grandmother," Tíaquena said aloud as she lifted her head toward the sacred mountain. "I will honor you tonight and strive to be my best. I promise to make you proud, and I hope to see you when the Zemí spirits and the spirits of our ancestors gather; it will be my great honor if you believe me worthy."

She knows the purpose of her dancing is to communicate with the spirits and the tribe's ancestors and bring messages back to Cacique. But Tíaquena's desire to see her grandmother again, is what gives her the strength and courage to face the danger and uncertainty.

"I will be brave, Grandmother," Tíaquena promises as she moves toward the village and her destiny. Years of practice have brought her to this moment. She knows the next few hours belong to her. She pauses one last time at the edge of the village, feeling the energy from Yuké rising inside her.

Tíaquena arrives at the village and enters the sacred space defined by the circle of stones. The tribe gathers around her. Ritual preparations, meditation, and a dose of cohoba powder from Cacique fuel her readiness for what lies ahead.

The Zemi spirits, tattooed on Tíaquena's body over the last several months, take on new meaning as the bom-bom-bom, bom-bom of the tambors and the shick, shick-a-shick of the maracas intensifies. With the addition of the shell and stone adornments, the soft trilling sound they produce during her dance will open the portal and pierce the veil separating her from the spirit world.

The beat of the maracas and the tambors quickens, and so does Tíaquena's dancing. She knows this is a critical moment.

Atabey cannot be angered for fear of unleashing her alter ego, Guabancex. Guabancex controls the hurricanes and floods, so Tíaquena knows how she performs will mean the difference between favor and punishment. Atabey, who controls the moon, life-giving water, and fertility, needs to be honored, enticed, and seduced.

She feels the circle collapsing around her in the grip of the tambours and maracas. Cacique lifts his scepter and utters the sacred words known only to him and past chiefs. The look in his eyes sends a shiver through Tíaquena, a mix of dread and excitement. She knows Atabey is close. The cohoba powder, Cacique's magic, and the tribe's exhortations open the door to the spirit world, and she senses herself being transported to the other side.

Atabey is now in control, drawing Tíaquena's spirit toward Yuké. The tribe continues moving in a faster, more urgent, undulating wave, pressing closer to the center of the circle and Tíaquena. Transformed into the vessel through which Atabey will communicate, it's time to ask the great and beautiful goddess for guidance. It is now on her to establish and maintain a spiritual connection to the other side.

Bom-bom-bom, bom-bom, shick, shick-a-shick . . .

Dancing with an urgency of purpose, knowing this is her moment of destiny, Tíaquena feels one more shiver. She lifts her head, looking at the light that is not the moon but Atabey's face. As she catches Atabey's gaze, her body convulses with her last conscious thought.

Naked and lithe, covered in sacred tattoos and adorned in ritual shells and stones, Tíaquena moves in a way that defies gravity and with an energy that flows up from the ground, through the mountain, and into her. She dances fearlessly into the night, not as Tíaquena but as the messenger of Atabey.

As the ceremony unfolds on shore, Christopher Columbus is asleep in his cabin, dreaming about the new world he's discovered and the fame and fortune it will bring him. The trip has already been successful, with the discovery of several Caribbean islands. Columbus claimed all of the newly discovered lands for Spain, and the fact that most of them were inhabited was of no consequence. He has little interest in the religious beliefs and practices of the Indigenous people he meets. In the years that follow, this fact will devastate those who live on the island and speak to their ancestors through elaborate and sacred ceremonies.

Tíaquena's dance of the sacred *Areyto* will mark the last time the tribe practices its religion unhindered by the invaders. The beliefs and practices of the Taíno will undergo significant changes, adapting to both the religious indoctrination of the Spaniards and the religions practiced by the Africans who will come later.

The *Areyto* is the one exception to this syncretization. This sacred ceremony will survive the next five hundred years and remain essential to Cuban religious practice.

Maximillian

— · ♦♦♦ · —

"You know that place between sleep and awake, where you still remember dreaming . . . ? That is where I'll be waiting."

— *James V. Hart, Hook*

My name is Maximillian Albury. I am a fourth-generation Conch, born and raised in Key West. My parents are Conchs, as are my grandparents, great-grandparents, and great-great-grandparents. Our relatives migrated from the Bahamas, from Green Turtle Cay to Key West in the late 1800s. Before that, they lived in South Carolina, tending farms and livestock and trading with those they knew in Europe.

We are Scotch-Irish with a sprinkling of Cuban on my father's side. His mother was Cuban, born in Guanabacoa, Cuba, and baptized in the church in Regla. The addition of Cuban blood does not affect my status as a Conch. It has something to do with the proximity of Key West to Cuba. The two islands are only ninety miles apart. All of these facts come into play as this story unfolds.

I met Julian Valladares online. We love telling the story of our meeting because it always raises eyebrows. I read the book Julian and his father wrote about his father's time at the Finca Vigía in San Francisco de Paula, Cuba. The Finca Vigía was Ernest Hemingway's home, and Ramón Valladares was Hemingway's majordomo for 16 years. Ramón saw that the household ran smoothly. He was the first person to see Hemingway in the morning when the author did most of his writing. It was Ramón's job to protect Hemingway from unwanted interruptions.

I was impressed with Ramón's story, so I contacted Julian to compliment him and his father on the book. We developed a friendship based on our interest in the writer and his connections to Key West and Cuba. Hemingway lived in both places, and our curiosity drove our interest in his experiences and how they influenced his writing.

We traveled to Cuba several times before the Hemingway Colloquium but this was our first official trip. The last day of the Colloquium was held at the Finca Vigía. When it concluded, we did not return to Havana with the rest of the participants. Instead, we walked from the Finca to his Aunt Nita's home. Julian had contacted his aunt, and she knew we were coming.

A few days after we returned from Cuba, I started having dreams about the visit. When the dream started, I wrote down what I remembered as soon as I awakened. As it repeated, I kept adding details I'd missed. Sometimes, I would wake in the middle of the night, turn on the small lamp beside my bed, and write as neatly as possible in a small, leather-bound journal. Other times, I would write in the morning. As the dream was repeating, those parts of the story I recorded during the daylight weren't any less dreamlike.

The things I learned in Julian's family home in San Francisco de Paula were real. I met his aunt and his cousins, nieces, and nephews. The experience didn't seem extraordinary then, even though I learned some extraordinary things. As the months passed, my memory of that day became tangled in the story unfolding in the dream. As it became more detailed, it was harder to sort what might be my imagination from reality. Eventually, it all merged.

Now, I think of that visit as the beginning. Some of what I wrote down is real; some may be my imagination. Either way, when the dreams came, and the story evolved, I could only start my day once I had filled in the blanks and added new parts.

Before the dream, I had never doubted the reality of that day and our visit to Finca Vigía and Aunt Nita's house. I have never doubted the truth of what happened next, how it affected me, and what it meant. Now that it has all blended, I don't try to separate the real from the imagined. With everything that has happened, I don't think it matters.

San Fransisco de Paula

"Max, this is the way Papa and my father walked to go into the pueblo," Julian says as we move through the gate and into the street.

It is a pilgrimage to cover the distance from the Finca to Aunt Nita's house. I've never come this way, but the walk seems familiar. The houses look the same as when Hemingway last saw them, a testament to the pride and endurance of the Cuban people. I'm struck by how powerful and grounded they are as they defy the weather and the odds.

I know Julian must be thinking about his father, but neither of us mentions him. As we walk, the streets are filled with people, and no one pays attention to the sidewalks. We pass several dogs looking gaunt and homeless, but I know from experience that none of the dogs in Cuba are homeless. They all belong to someone, or they belong to everyone.

The dogs, the people, and the shadows all move in the same slow, deliberate way. It has the feel of choreography, and the rhythm of this dance embraces us. It isn't long before we blend in, becoming one with the rhythm and the energy of the people around us. Our sense of reality resets to a different frequency, and we both feel it.

I sense spirits in the shadows as the sun moves toward the horizon. They are here to transport us, and we walk from the present into the past without feeling out of time and place.

Being surrounded by this energy, enhanced by both the rhythm of the island and the people, generates a sense of comfort.

The streets remind me of growing up in Key West, and I realize that is why everything seems so familiar. I grew up on streets lined with modest houses, much like the streets and homes in San Francisco de Paula. I think about how much history Key West and Cuba share, ninety miles apart on either side of the Gulf Stream. The similarities remind us of the connection between the two islands.

As we walk, several people wave and say hello. Julian is dressed in white, so I know that those people who are out on the street recognize him as a Palo Priest. It's not the first time I've noticed how Cubans look at him.

We are greeted with great affection when we arrive at Aunt Nita's. Julian's aunt and cousins welcomed me like family.

When we visited before, we stayed in two front rooms, a living/dining room, and a small kitchen. This time, we move toward the back, passing several rooms and ending up on a covered patio area serving as an outdoor kitchen, dining room, and ritual space.

One of Julian's cousins, Pepe, greets us as we move outside. He tells us he is making three thousand ham croquets, or "*croquetas.*" He is moving swiftly and deliberately. The process looks haphazard and planned at the same time. At any given time, at least four family members help, sometimes as many as six.

The sun has set, and the cicadas are singing. The cousins, nieces, and nephews each take part in one of the steps needed to make the *croquetas*. This process continues with constant unrelated conversations, and it doesn't look like anyone is focused on their job. The discussion is wide-ranging, and Julian translates so I can follow along.

I think about the supply of raw materials used to make ham *croquetas*. Pepe explains that ham is the biggest challenge. The secret ham ingredient in these *croquetas* is Goya canned ham. I know you can't buy Goya canned ham in Cuba. When I mention this, Pepe smiles and tells me the ham comes from Miami, carried by an assortment of friends who function as "mules." I'm impressed with the ingenuity in creating this Cuban food staple, and I'm reminded again how Cubans adapt to almost any circumstance and survive.

A light rain starts to fall and, within a few minutes, turns into a hard downpour, battering the roof overhead. The sound of the cicadas is replaced by the soothing sound of rain on a tin roof.

As the work on the *croquetas* continues, Julian invites me to the back of the house, past the outdoor kitchen. There are several small rooms, and he motions me to peek into one of the enclosed spaces, empty except for a small iron cauldron. The iron pot, called a *Nganga*, contains various items. Pepe is a Ngangulero, and It's a privilege to see this space. I'm struck by how sacred it feels.

"What does a Ngangulero do?" I ask.

"Nganga refers to the Palo religion's practice and the practitioner. Pepe oversees the spiritual needs of the neighborhood," Julian says. "He consults with Aunt Nita. She is the *Nana Nganga* of our family's *munansos* or religious community. The two of them are respected among the practitioners and the believers. Everyone is connected to a *munansos* whose religious history is kept as a sort of communal memory."

"So, your family consists of several Palo priests and practitioners?" I ask. "I assume this includes your father."

"Yes," Julian says, handing me some dark rum. "Pepe has been practicing for some time under the watchful eye of Aunt Nita. Our *munansos*, or house, consists of many people in the neighborhood. Some practice, but most are believers and come to Pepe and my aunt for advice, protection, and healing. It's what my father used to do when he lived here."

Julian leads me past the outdoor kitchen, back into the house, and up the stairs to several bedrooms. There are altars in the corners or along an entire wall. Moving through the rooms brings me closer to my heritage and my Cuban family, who lived near Guanabacoa. My link to Cuban spirituality is through my grandmother, my father's mother. It's a connection I suspected and confirmed on my second trip to Havana. On that trip, we visited the church in Regla where my great-grandmother was baptized.

These altars remind me of my grandmother's house in Key West. There was a parlor where she displayed these kinds of vessels, figurines, and objects. I didn't know what the significance was at the time, and she never gave any explanation. Being in these rooms gives me the same sensation I experienced in Guanabacoa. But these are not museum displays; these are actual altars.

When we return to the outside seating area, the *croquetas* are still coming off the assembly line in a never-ending dance of creation, deep-frying, and packaging. Questions swirl in my head. Was my great-grandfather a devotee of Inlé, the *Orisha* of healing? How connected was my great-grandmother to religion, having been baptized in the church in Regla? How did my grandmother continue the tradition of the faith, and why did she never discuss this part of our history with any of the family?

The rum I've been sipping begins to work its magic, and the rain has settled into a slow, steady thrumming. We aren't back long before Aunt Nita announces dinner is ready.

Communion

Cubans eat close to the land. The black beans and rice, the pork, and the yuca combine in flavor, texture, and color in a way that can't be described, only experienced. The smell of the food inside the house is intoxicating. Blending the garlic, olive oil, turmeric, oregano, and other ingredients is done with a balance that respects the food, the family's history, and the culture. There is a reverence for the food here on the outskirts of Havana, and I know I am being treated to a bounty the family rarely sees. As a guest, I am offered the best they can assemble, and I know Julian has helped with the cost.

Aunt Nita presided over the offering, and the meal celebrated the food and the family. There is no letup in the conversation, and the festive atmosphere continues until everyone has had what they want to eat. The family has had a professional chef for one or two generations, and the food attests to this. It is spectacular.

We have had an eventful afternoon and evening, and now it is time for us to return to Havana. Another cousin arrives in a green Plymouth to take us back to the city. Javier is a mountain of a man who barely fits into the front seat of the 1955 Plymouth. His demeanor belies his size as he respects Julian and me, letting us know he appreciates the opportunity to drive us back to Havana. Julian's nephew rides with us to keep us company on the way back.

The rain has washed the streets, and the reflection off the wet pavement adds to the surreal ending of the evening. The distance from San Francisco de Paula to Havana is not far, but the roads make the trip challenging. Julian is translating the conversation, and I learn that Javier lives nearby and makes a living doing odd jobs around the pueblo. This is how he has come to own the car. The story of coming into ownership of a car in Cuba is told with great detail. We listen carefully because owning a car in Cuba can mean the difference between survival and struggle.

The light is faint now, and the streets alternate between a soft white glow and the sepia glow so familiar in Havana. The light and shadows define the journey. Before long, we are back at the Plaza de Armas.

We say goodbye to Javier and Julian's nephew and begin our walk back to our rooms on O'Reilly Street. The night is warm and humid, as is often the case in Havana. The streets are wet from a rainstorm that has dampened the city but not its mood.

Our rooms are in a house owned by a concert violinist. We hope she is still up as we open the front door and enter the foyer. Instead, we find a bottle of rum and two glasses with a note:

Dear Julian and Max,

I am sorry I cannot visit you tonight; my responsibilities call me elsewhere. I am disappointed I won't hear about your day. Please accept this rum in my absence. In the morning, tell me if you think this bottle was a fair substitute for my company.

Love, Ileana

Julian picks up the bottle, a Havana Club Añejo, aged twelve years, and pours two shots. He lifts his glass and gestures to me to take a sip. We move to a small sitting room. It is late, and the streets have quieted, so the room is silent except for the ticking of a large mantle clock in the dining room.

"That was a lot to take in, Amigo," I say to Julian, who looks deep in thought.

"I wanted you to see it," he says. "The Palo religion goes back generations in my family."

"I know your father is a Palo priest," I say.

"Yes, he practiced here on the island and now in New Jersey."

"Are you a priest?" Julian knows the question is coming, and he smiles.

"My father is training me in the ways of Palo Monte, but the process is slow under the best of circumstances. It's hard to progress outside of Cuba. For someone like me, the best way to describe it is that I am on a path to understanding, like many other religions. I am an initiate."

As we sit and sip rum, I wonder what secrets Julian keeps and how long it will take him to trust me. I wonder if he will ever trust me with secrets that go back hundreds of years.

Reflecting on the end of that day, I am struck by how little I knew about Julian, his father, and their religion. Cubans are complicated, and I was beginning to understand their complexity.

Without Ileana's company, the evening ends. It will be two years before we plan another trip to Havana. The island remained the same during our absence, but everything related to Julian's life and journey changed. The changes were not slow and subtle but quick and life-altering.

Julian

—·—·····—·—

The Nfumbe "vibes" through the Nganga, but he doesn't live there; he is everywhere and nowhere.

— Oscar Guerrero

To practice Palo Monte is to connect with personal lineages. In ritual practices, references in songs and dialogues among the practitioners produce the religious importance of people's passage, power, and personage. Invoking religious ritual language creates meaning and capacities to identify Congo spirits, Cuban Congo ancestry, and a Cuban Congo identity. The veneration of recently passed family members, the salutations of past ancestors, the control, attraction, and exploitation of human spirits, and the interaction and counsel of the dead are all at play in the lives of Nganguleros and Nganguleras.

— Lonn S. Monroe

Nfumbe

It was the middle of December, and the darkness and the cold had come to Union City, New Jersey, without apology or remorse. Ramón had been dead for two months, and Julian had not dreamt of him. As a Ngangulero in the Palo Monte religion, Ramón should have been communicating with his son, who was also his initiate. Dreams are essential in the Palo religion to provide guidance and comfort for the living. Without them, there is only confusion and doubt. The lack of contact left Julian uncertain about his father's journey to the afterlife.

"Where are you, old man?" Julian said aloud as he stood in his studio painting an image of two Cuban fishermen. Over the past several weeks, he had been trying to speak to his father while painting.

"Why are you ignoring me?" Julian asked again aloud.

He was frowning and had stopped painting. Instead of focusing on the image on the canvas, he was staring at Ramón's *Nganga*, the heavy iron cauldron, sitting in the corner of the studio. The relic looked as it did the day Ramón died. Julian had been careful not to disturb anything it held for fear of upsetting his father's journey to the afterlife. At first, the large iron pot had been a comfort. Now, it was mocking him.

The suddenness of Ramón's death created insurmountable complications for Julian. The passing of a Palo priest in Cuba demands elaborate funeral rituals that blend African, Catholic, and Indigenous traditions. In addition, as repositories of sacred knowledge and practices, it is essential that before their death, priests pass on their expertise to chosen successors. When a death is sudden, the priest's inability to formally name a successor can interrupt the religious hierarchy of the living and the transition of the dead priest to the other side. In these cases, communication with spirits—often called *nfumbe* or *muertos*—becomes a central aspect of the ceremony. Special chants and rituals open the connection between the two worlds and ensure a smooth transition from the world of the living to the afterlife. Without them, the newly departed may wander somewhere in between, burdened by unfinished business and unsure where they belong. In Ramón's case, there had been no special ceremony, and Julian worried that his father would be unable to complete his journey.

As his father's undeclared successor, Julian's journey from initiate to priest should have been accomplished under Ramón's tutelage. But it was a slow and deliberate process carried out in small steps over many years. Now, the journey had been interrupted, and the lack of communication from his father was only amplifying Julian's sense of loss and confusion.

Julian returned his focus to the canvas and the images he was creating. The Cuban fishermen carried fish on a pole propped on their shoulders. The men were old and weathered, neither smiling nor frowning. Staring out at Julian with pleading looks, both men were hunched and tired. They were also facing in opposite directions, their backs to each other. The problem was the point.

Julian's friends and family had been left to worry about his state of mind as he worked for weeks in isolation. Instead of reaching out, he had turned inward, convinced painting would lead him to his father. So far, the strategy hadn't worked.

The *nganga* broke Julian's concentration, and he knew he was done painting for the evening. He would try again tomorrow, to capture the loneliness and isolation of being stuck between two worlds without your father—your mentor.

The paintings of the two fishermen would stretch into weeks and then months. Julian's work flourished during this time, and the old fishermen revealed themselves in many ways. The paintings always had a sense of freedom, structure, and restrictions. The old men were always looking toward the horizon without any means of escape. The paintings reflected the Cuban dilemma—an endless horizon and isolation.

Julian painted during the day and sometimes into the night. When he slept, he dreamt, but the dreams were of familiar places and people he had known or still knew. There were childhood dreams, and sometimes, his father was in them. But they were always in the past. They reminded him of his life as a young boy and his relationship with his parents. There was never anything new. Never anything from the other side. Nothing from Ramón. But that was about to change.

Twilight

It's the middle of July, and Julian is dreaming about Cuba. In this dream, the orioles are singing, and the morning light, filtering through the mango trees, is bright enough to reveal the yellow patches on their shoulders and under their wings. The brash sound of the orioles is mixed with the cooing of the mourning doves landing on the terrace. The air is thick with tropical moisture, and the Pueblo of San Francisco de Paula is starting to stir. Julian can smell the mangoes. He can also smell the coffee roasting in the small roaster outside the fence encircling the Finca Vigía property. Several years ago, someone in the pueblo acquired a small commercial roasting machine, and they were fast at work roasting and packaging beans.

This is one of his usual dreams, and he knows how it ends. The familiarity is comforting, and he waits for it to play out. Then he hears his father's voice, and everything changes. A surge of electricity passes through him. There is a moment when he thinks he has awakened, but he is still asleep:

"*Tú sabes lo que tienes que hacer*—you know what you must do," Ramón says firmly.

After months of waiting, Ramón appeared shirtless and barefoot, wearing faded, worn-out blue jeans. He looks as he did when he was fifty, with a dark salt and pepper mustache, solid and well-defined arms and chest, and a narrow waist. After he speaks, he stands staring at Julian for a long time as if he doesn't know what to do next.

Ramón isn't alone. A woman in a long, flowing, white dress with a white turban headdress stands beside him. She is wearing wide-loop earrings and gold bracelets on both wrists. Her eyes are dark and penetrating. She's smiling, with full, red lips revealing several gold teeth.

The three of them are on a side terrace of the main house. Ramón gives Julian a big smile and then turns serious again.

"*Tú sabes lo que tienes que hacer*—you know what you must do," he repeats.

Julian stares at the woman and looks back at his father. Ramón is younger now. He appears as Julian remembers him at age forty. His arms are up around his chest as if he has a chill.

"It is not cold. We are in Cuba," Julian says, "*estamos en la Finca. We are at the Finca.*"

The woman is a Palo priestess, but Julian doesn't know why she is there.

"*Tú sabes lo que tienes que hacer,*" Ramón says for the third time, and Julian wants to ask his father what he means; he tries to ask but can't speak.

The priestess and the Finca grounds fade away. Now, Ramón and Julian are standing and facing each other.

"*Go now and find the darkness,*" Ramón says as he disappears. "*Go and find the way.*"

The dream ends, and Julian rolls over and turns on the light beside his bed. It hums softly as the pull chain clicks against the painted ceramic finish. He is sure his father hasn't transitioned to the other side and that he is somehow to blame. While the Palo religion doesn't recognize the concept of purgatory, this is how he thinks of his father's existence—trapped between the living and the dead in perpetual darkness.

Julian sits up to clear his mind and remembers the Hemingway Colloquium. He and I will be in Havana tomorrow. It isn't hard to connect his father's appearance to the timing.

Being in Havana will allow him to explore the one ritual he knows can help his father find his place in the afterlife. It's the only way he knows to communicate with those on the other side. The challenge will be to find someone on the island who is powerful enough to assemble the necessary participants and willing to try.

The phone rings and startles him. It's 4 a.m., and he knows it's his wake-up call.

"Good morning, Max," Julian says, answering the phone.

"Wake up, Amigo!" I say, sounding cheerful. "I will see you in Orlando in a few hours. We are going to have a great time."

"We are indeed!" Julian says. "I will see you in Orlando."

Julian stands, hesitates for a moment, and walks toward the bathroom. Seeing his father in his dreams had changed everything. The trip to Havana has now taken on a new meaning and purpose. It is going to be much more complicated.

Havana

———·•◆·•·———

SUNDAY

Mirage

The Hemingway Colloquium is held every other year in Havana. The Cuban Cultural Affairs Commission schedules its conference in the off years, so it doesn't compete with the International Hemingway Conference. This year, it starts on Tuesday and runs for three days.

I met Julian in Orlando as planned. We were booked on an early afternoon flight, scheduled to arrive at the Jose Martí Airport around 2 p.m. When I saw him, I knew something wasn't right. He seemed distracted and worried.

"Are you okay?" I asked.

He paused for a moment, trying to decide what to say.

"I'm fine," he said.

He left it at that, and I decided not to press. I knew he would tell me if there was something he wanted me to know.

The flight was on time, and after gathering our bags and clearing customs at the Jose Marti Airport, we took a taxi to the Elita apartments in Vedado. When we arrived, we showed our passports to the doorman, Emilio, who showed us to our apartment on the fourth floor. It was clean and nicely appointed. The bathrooms were small but modern, and the air-conditioning was cold.

We were anxious to return to Old Havana, so after dropping our bags, we went downstairs, where Julian hailed a taxi and directed the driver to the Plaza de Armas. It is the oldest plaza in Havana and is always busy with book vendors selling books, posters, and other memorabilia on the revolution, Fidel Castro, Che Guevara, and the island's history.

From there, we walk toward Havana Harbor. The Gulf Stream is running close to shore with waves rolling in and crashing against the seawall. As we make our way on the boulevard, around the opening of the harbor, across from El Morro, the sun is casting bright light on the facades of the buildings as it moves toward the horizon.

People crowd the seawall, mostly young couples, some fishermen, and a sprinkling of tourists. The restored buildings, the ones with new glass windows, reflected the light toward the ocean in defiance, having been recently reclaimed from the constant assault of the wind and salt spray. It felt good to see the boulevard coming back to life.

The Malecón is the perfect place to discuss the connection between Key West and Cuba. The idea of a connection between the two islands had been part of our conversation since we first met. It started with discussions about Ernest Hemingway, but we both knew the connection between the two islands existed well before Hemingway—that it was part of what he discovered, not what he created. Being on the Malecón, looking north toward Key West, made it real.

Several ideas exist about how the connection manifests itself. One suggests you can see the glow of lights from Havana and Key West halfway across the Gulf Stream. A second popular theory is that you can see the Sand Key Lighthouse from Havana when the conditions are right. Of course, the definition of the right conditions is always up for discussion.

Another claim we discussed was seeing Havana from Key West as a vision or mirage suspended above the Gulf Stream as a moving picture. This one was supported by a newspaper article printed in the Key West Citizen in 1934.

> **Many Key Westers see a vision of Havana reflected in the sky:** Shortly after 6 o'clock last Friday, there gradually appeared a peculiar-looking haze about three miles above the horizon and just as though it was a moving picture where the spirit-like semblance of a scene or persons gradually appears, the city of Havana loomed before the astonished and awe-struck gaze of the watchers.

"It's a myth," I said. "You can't see Havana from Key West or Key West from Havana, standing here at night or any other time."

"This article says shortly after 6 o'clock. Wouldn't it still be light?" Julian asks.

"Yes, I think so," I said. "Probably close to dusk in May."

"It's ninety miles to Key West from here, right?" He asked.

"Yes, and the horizon is only three miles. It's three miles to the horizon," I said, pointing toward Key West. "Then everything disappears."

"I know," Julian said. Looking at the article, he read the following paragraph:

> Not only was the picture there, it is stated, but buildings could be discerned and recognized. The Presidential Palace could be seen, and other buildings, such as the Morro Castle and Hotel Plaza, were easily recognized. Even pedestrians

and vehicles were seen on the streets, and the Prado was crowded. One of the watchers was convinced he was looking at a miracle and was inclined to believe that some startling news of Cuba would soon be given to the world.

I thought for a long time before answering. "I don't know Julian," I said. "I still don't think you'll ever see buildings and people. Besides, no one has ever claimed to see a Key West mirage from Cuba."

He thought for a moment. "It would be nice if we could," he said, with more than a hint of disappointment.

I knew Julian had done the research. When the mirage appeared in Key West, Hemingway owned *Pilar* for over a week. On the afternoon of the event, he was fishing off the coast of Cuba with Joe Russell and a few others. It was the first of many trips to Havana. I wondered if Julian considered that connection, but I didn't ask. I didn't want to press the point.

"It's been over sixty years since the United States placed the embargo on Cuba," Julian said. "That means anyone who can remember how the two islands connected would be in their '70s or '80s. We are a couple of generations removed from understanding how close they are."

"This is the point, isn't it?" I asked. "It's ninety miles, and that distance is smaller now than when the U.S. cut travel. With the new boats and modern technology, traversing the Gulf Stream would be nothing. I agree. No one knows how close they are."

Stopped in front of the old Hotel Deauville, we were looking north toward Key West when a large swell rolled in and crashed over the sea wall. A fisherman tried to dodge the spray, but two young couples stood firm. Embracing each other and welcoming the salt water, they smiled and laughed as it came over them.

In the commotion, three white crowned pigeons startled, took flight, and headed south toward Old Havana. Their presence, and the fact there were three of them, was an omen for Julian.

"We should go," he said. He hailed a taxi, and we headed back to the apartment.

As we accelerate from the curb into traffic, I see a sculpture of a woman cast in steel. Windswept, with the features of her face in full resolution, the concrete pedestal she sits on is anchored to the floor of a demolished building. The contrast is jarring; she looks out of place but unfazed by her surroundings. Staring north across the Florida Straits, she appears to be looking for something or someone. I get a sense of anticipation and yearning, but it may be my perspective and not the artist's intention.

I want to warn her that no matter how hard she concentrates, the horizon is only three miles.

Three miles to the horizon, and then everything disappears.

On Top
of the World

We were headed back to Old Havana for dinner, and I suggested a cigar afterward. I was uneasy about Julian's mood, and I thought a cigar and some rum after dinner might be an excellent way to find out what was bothering him.

As we approached the drop-off point, Julian asked if I was up for pizza.

"There's this place I remember from last time," he said. "It's at the corner of O'Reilly and San Ignacio."

"You know I'm not fond of the pizza in Cuba, right?" I said.

I was prepared to lose this battle, but I didn't want to go down without a fight. My strategy was to let him get it out of his system so we wouldn't have to eat Cuban pizza when Phoebe and Mera arrived.

"I think this will be better than what we are used to," he said.

"I'm willing to give it a try," I said. "As long as you think it's going to be better than the usual."

I could see by the look on his face that Julian had no idea why I had any qualms about Cuban pizza.

We sat inside, in the air-conditioning, and ate a cheese and ham pizza. It turned out to be a typical Cuban pizza, which smelled and tasted too intense, thanks to the cheese peculiar to the island. Nevertheless, Julian was thrilled by the whole experience, and I paid the dues, not only for me but for Mera and Phoebe as well.

After dinner, we walked down San Ignacio and turned left onto Obispo. The Ambos Mundos was a couple of blocks down Obispo, on the right. We walked into the side entrance to the elevator and asked the elevator attendant to take us to the rooftop bar.

The sky was clear, with a breeze off the ocean. We found a comfortable spot on the outer edge of the roof, at the northeast corner. We had a view of the Plaza de Armas, past Santa Isabel and the church with the Ceiba tree, and past that, across the harbor to the fort. We ordered two double shots of Havana Club rum on the way to the chairs, and the waiter followed us and set them on the table. Julian's favorite cigars were Romeo and Julieta; the two he had with him were packaged in metal tubes to keep them fresh. I had the cutter and the lighter, so we made a good team.

We touched glasses and took a sip of the rum.

"You go first," I said. I handed Julian the cutter and the lighter. He unscrewed the cap and carefully slid the cigar out between his fingers. He inspected the cigar for blemishes or holes. Finding none, he put the cigar under his nose and sniffed it.

"How is it?" I asked.

"It's very nice," he said.

Julian took the cutter and carefully cut off the end, making sure he didn't dislodge the cap. He drew on the cigar to test it.

"How is it?" I asked again, meaning the draw and the taste.

"It has a nice draw," he said.

He flicked open the cap of the lighter and held the flame to the end of the cigar. The tip started to glow red, and I watched as the cigar smoke lifted into the air.

When Julian was done, I lit my cigar.

"It doesn't get any better than this, Amigo," Julian said as he took a draw on the cigar and followed up with a sip of rum. The smoke lifted into the air in defiance of the light breeze from the water. "The only thing missing is my father's totem. We could share some rum and a cigar with him if it were here. He always loved his rum and cigars."

When we smoked at Julian's house, he always blew some cigar smoke onto the totem. It was part of the ritual.

"I'm sorry I never met him," I said.

"You would have liked him," Julian said. "And he would have liked you. He already did like you even though he never met you."

I drew on the cigar, slowly letting the smoke escape from my mouth. I watched it rise above the wall. It was blue against the light on the patio as it hovered for a long time between us.

"How do you know?" I asked.

"Remember the first time we met? He wanted me to deliver one of the Hemingway photos to you."

"I remember," I said. "You made a point of telling me your father wanted me to have it."

"He did want you to have it, but he told me to make sure I wanted you to have it also."

"I see," I said, smiling. "So, it was an audition. And apparently, I passed because you gave me the photograph."

"Yes, you passed," Julian said, smiling. "My father was thrilled that it all worked out for me. Look where it has gotten us. Can you believe we are sitting atop the Ambos Mundos, smoking Cuban cigars and drinking Cuban rum? Look at this view. Hemingway fell in love with this view and wrote about it. He saw almost exactly what we are seeing now."

We sat silently for a moment, savoring the cigars and the rum. The cigar's nutty aftertaste paired nicely with the Havana Club, and the smoke settled around us.

"It has been quite an adventure, my friend," I said. "Look at all the things we have done and the places we have been."

I paused for a moment, taking another sip of rum.

"But I have a question for you and want an honest answer. Is this adventure about to end?"

The waiter walked over with a bottle of Havana Club and refilled our glasses. The sun had set, and music played softly in the far corner. In the distance, we could see El Morro and the castle, with its lighted Cuban flag flying from the tower. The breeze had died down, and the smoke from the cigars was now hanging between us. It was a perfect night, and the view of the Old City was as intoxicating as ever.

Over the past three years, Julian and I have spent hours in conversations like this. We talk about everything from the meaning of life to the importance of Julian's work, Hemingway's work, and mine. It is always over rum and cigars. Most of the time, his father's totem sits between us as if Ramón is listening to the conversations. I always assume he is. Tonight, it feels especially likely.

"I don't know what you mean," Julian said, taking a long, hard look at me.

"Something is not right," I said. "Something is a little off with you, and I'm not sure what it is."

Julian sat still, drawing on his cigar and sipping rum. He gazed out across the rooftops of Old Havana, deep in thought. The sound of conversation from some of the closer tables became more pronounced, and I followed Julian's gaze across the tops of the buildings surrounding the hotel. I waited for him to gather his thoughts, following his lead with my cigar and a sip of rum.

The smoke was still thick between us, and Ramón's presence was palpable now. The band had just finished a break and was playing in the far corner. It was a sultry Cuban song, and I recognized it immediately—"Chan-Chan."

"I have been struggling lately with the loss of my parents, my father in particular, since he was my spiritual mentor," Julian said after a long pause. "This is to take nothing away from my mother. I loved her very much. But the fact that my father is no longer available to me has been weighing on me for some time."

"Isn't there someone else you can turn to?" I asked. "Is there anyone back home or here on the island?"

"It's not that simple," Julian said. "My father traced his ancestry back to Baracoa and the ancient Taíno on his mother's side and to Africa on his father's side. The family history included a spirituality that fused the Caribbean with the African and then adapted in ways dictated by the invasion of the Spanish and their introduction of Catholicism. Baracoa was the first place Columbus landed on the island of Cuba. Stories had been carried for generations about the intermingling of religious practices. This is the tradition of *munansos*, or a sense of community, which is nuanced. The Palo religious practices exist in these social and cultural frameworks."

Julian took another draw on his cigar, and for a long while, we sat in silence.

"Max, if we talk about this, I need you to listen to me and not make judgments. It's funny that you and I have only known each other briefly, yet our friendship has become so meaningful to me."

"You know I feel the same way," I said. "Please understand; anything you tell me stays between us. But don't say anything that will make you uncomfortable. Please know I'm here for you whenever you want to share or whatever you want me to do."

I watched him pause again. I could see him calculating what to tell me and what to keep to himself.

"Today on the Malecón, I felt my father's presence," Julian said, breaking his silence. "It was the strongest I had felt him since he passed. It might have been the waves rolling in and the light. When we were about to leave, the three white crowned pigeons that took flight were a sign to me that he was there. I won't go into the details, but seeing those birds, the ocean, and the sky made me feel like he was close. In some strange way, that's why the idea of seeing one island from the other is so important to me. I know it doesn't have any connection, but it's the idea that things happen here. The idea that extraordinary things can happen, like mirages and other unexplainable or unusual things. It suggests a connection to the other world."

"I understand," I said.

"Standing out there convinced me to try and do what I can to ease my mind and pain."

"What would that be?"

"To answer your previous question, yes, there are people here on the island that can help. The problem is I'm not sure how to find them. Watching the waves crash over the sea wall and seeing the reaction of the fishermen and the young couples, each was different, but each acknowledged the power of the sea and the current. At that moment, I realized I would get my answers here. The people that can help are powerful, spiritual people, Max. They are Shamans or priests and priestesses, for lack of better words, who can put me in touch with those on the other side. My father talked about it often. It all sounds preposterous when I explain it, but their rituals have existed for centuries. They have been protected and performed for generations, passed down carefully from one person to the next."

"How will you go about finding these people?" I asked.

"Since I can no longer access my father's friends, I think my best opportunity is in Regla. I know it's a long shot, but I feel the pull somehow of a pilgrimage to the church to make a connection. I feel it, and I can't explain why."

"Is there any way I can help?" I asked.

"You can keep my intentions and my feelings to yourself. I don't want Phoebe and Mera to know anything about this until I'm ready to explain it."

"You have my word," I said. "There isn't anything to explain. You haven't found anyone."

"Exactly," Julian said. "Even if or when I do, there may still be things I don't want to discuss."

"It's up to you, Amigo. I promise I won't betray your confidence."

We both fell silent again. Sitting on top of the Ambos Mundos, it was easy to feel like all our problems could be solved with the right cigar and some Cuban rum. But as I sat watching Julian enjoying his Romeo and Julieta, I couldn't help but think his challenge was immense. He hadn't told me what he was trying to do, keeping the details to himself. I respected his privacy.

I didn't want him to feel cornered, so I changed the subject.

"You know, Julian, that day we visited your aunt's house was extraordinary for me," I said. "It was symbolic and real at the same time."

"What was the symbolism?" he asked.

"That's easy. It was moving from the front of the house to the back," I said. "It was like pulling back layers. The farther back we journeyed, the closer I came to the truth of who you are. I also felt a strong connection to who I am. I didn't expect to have that kind of experience. It took me by surprise."

"I wanted you to see the reality of my religion, my father's religion," Julian said. "From then on, you knew where I was coming from."

"It was a start," I said. "I don't pretend to know much about the true nature of the Palo religion, but I think I know how deep it runs here on the island."

"What was real?" Julian asked.

"That part is not so easy," I said. "There is always an undercurrent to reality here on the island. It's not about the culture and the art. It's more about the way Cubans approach their reality. There is a deep foundation of spirituality. Not everyone practices the same religion, and I get that. But there is a sense of synchronicity, of synergy."

"It's not so simple, Max," Julian said.

"I know," I said. "I didn't mean to try and make it like it was. I know I will never fully understand how religion fits into the culture and the outlook of the Cubans. Not even with a teacher like you."

"You are right to feel that way," Julian said. "Sometimes I feel the same way because I left the island so young. I think that's part of what fuels my desperation. It's a big part of my desire to understand better and feel more of what is happening here on the island. I feel like my father's death stole a large part of that understanding from me. In general, the exiles feel a sense of loss of place. But the more acute loss is the sense of belonging, connection to a deeper spiritual energy, and separation from its source."

"I'm sorry you are struggling with this," I said. "You know I will help however I can."

"My father worked for Hemingway for 16 years," Julian said. "I know you remember his title."

"I do," I said. "It was Majordomo."

"Yes," Julian said. "Do you know what that means in English?"

"It means butler," I said. "Or something close to that."

"It has another meaning," Julian said, sounding conspiratorial. "My father was an initiate of Palo when he worked for Hemingway. The title Majordomo refers to a level of progression in the Palo Monte religious group or family."

"So, what's the other meaning?" I asked.

"Steward," Julian said. "My father was the steward of Hemingway's journey and his house."

At that moment, I realized Julian's story had so many angles that I had no hope of understanding how they all came together.

"You said Hemingway came in from fishing early on May 21, 1934, the day of the vision," Julian said. "What did he do the rest of the day?"

"According to the *Pilar* log, he worked," I said.

"What was he working on?" Julian asked.

"He had started *Green Hills of Africa*," I said.

"See?" Julian said, smiling.

I smiled back, but I didn't see. Looking back, I realize Julian had already made all the connections. All I could do was struggle to understand and keep up.

I put my cigar in the ashtray and took the last sip of rum. Julian did the same and told the bartender we were ready to settle. The smoke had cleared, and the rooftop was clear and breezy again. It was as if a spell had broken.

Amidst cigars and Cuban rum on the Ambos Mundos hotel roof, the universe orchestrated Julian's fate. Had I possessed the "gift" to sense the mystical, I might have read the swirling smoke's message, a foreboding shroud clinging to the moment. Taking a hand in sealing his fate, Julian sought an unknown figure on the island, convinced of their existence. Unbeknownst to us that night, the person Julian sought was also looking for him. The unfolding of destiny's intricate dance had begun.

MONDAY

———·◆·———·

Caridad

Caridad Arango, dressed in white with a white turban headdress, waits patiently at the gate in Orlando for her flight home. A powerful Palo priestess, she is known as a "Practitioner" or "*Ngangulera*" in Cuba.

Caridad is the head of her *munansos* or House in Guanabacoa. In the past, she would have been known, variously, as a "*Tatanganga*," Witchdoctor," or "Informant." Some, if not all, of these designations, carried the stain of colonialism and occupation and the curse of enslavement.

While her trip to Miami and Orlando to visit relatives was sometimes overwhelming, Caridad met practitioners in both places. Anywhere the Cuban diaspora had taken hold, the religion thrived. After over five hundred years of trying, the invaders and the slave traders were unsuccessful in eliminating the ancient ways and customs.

The Palo and Santeria religions and their offshoots had been so artfully embedded in the religious practices and iconography of Christianity that they couldn't be separated. Without knowing the signs or the differences, it was impossible to discourage the indigenous and African beliefs. Caridad was the perfect example of how religious culture and practices were preserved. Sometimes, the knowledge and the responsibility felt like a burden. This was one of those times.

Caridad understands the differences between practices and practitioners. Her world is less concerned with ancient practices and more with African and Afro-Cuban culture and traditions. As a contemporary Practitioner, she has always walked a fine line between ancient cults and culture and the practice of incantations and spells to achieve balance with the universe.

Like Julian's father, Caridad's practice of Palo Monte centers around a *Nganga*. She maintains her connection to the physical world and objects to accomplish desired outcomes. Like all other Palo practitioners, Caridad relies on dream interpretation, using the symbolism they reveal to navigate the uncertainties of the universe.

Over the past several weeks, she has been experiencing the same mysterious dream. It started in Guanabacoa and has come to her every night since, following her to Miami and Orlando where she has spent the last three days visiting relatives and friends.

This dream starts at the Finca Vigía with a father and a son. The old man exists in the afterlife, and the young man, the son, is alive.

Caridad's purpose is clear, keeping the son's focus on the father. The father looks cold when he appears, shivering with his arms wrapped around himself.

"It's not cold. We are in Cuba," the son says, *"estamos en la Finca."*

Caridad is unsure what the location of Ernest Hemingway's home—the Finca Vigía, has to do with anything.

The father smiles, and Caridad can see he recognizes his surroundings as he lowers his arms from his chest. The three of them are standing on a side terrace of the main house.

Suddenly, the father's look turns serious. *"Tú sabes lo que tienes que hacer—you know what you must do,"* he says firmly.

Caridad can see that the father is concerned.

"Tú sabes lo que tienes que hacer," the father says again.

She can't tell if the father is talking to the son, her, or both.

As the dream starts to fade, she hears the father make one more warning.

"Remember the darkness," he says.

Caridad has spent her lifetime interpreting dreams. Even though this dream is ambiguous, one thing is clear: she is being called to help. She knows she must search for the two men and find answers about why the father is reaching out. Since the old man has gone to the other side, Caridad will focus on the son. But where is he, and how can she find him?

"You know what you have to do."

The old man's warning haunts her as she waits at the gate in Orlando for the flight back to Havana.

The voice on the loudspeaker calls for boarding. Caridad gathers her belongings and heads to the gangway.

Vert-de-Gris

"Preparing a power object, a Nganga or amulet, is a serious endeavor and remains guarded among practitioners."

— *Lonn S. Monroe*

Fifteen minutes into the flight from Orlando to Havana, Mera Stadler's mind was in Paris. The International Hemingway Conference at the American University was a year ago. Now, on her way to the Hemingway Colloquium in Havana with Phoebe Brennan, she barely had time to catch her breath. Paris had exceeded her expectations. Now, in a whirlwind, she was on a flight to Cuba. It felt like a dream, but she was ready to embrace it.

Paris was where she, Phoebe, Max, and Julian had forged a bond around Hemingway studies. It was more than a bond. They had become fast friends during and after the experience. The conference was spectacular, and the "City of Light" was everything it was advertised to be. Passions had run high, but the conference ended, and each went their separate ways. Moving on never seemed like an option, and the Colloquium presented a perfect way to reconnect.

Peering out the window, Mera saw the Florida Keys slicing into the Gulf of Mexico. A tapestry of light greens revealed shallow banks, sandy bottoms, and coral reefs, contrasting with deeper blue-purple where the Gulf Stream's current flowed. Over the centuries, southeasterly winds had sculpted the scene, pushing sand and sediment northwest in broad strokes. The string of islands looked in motion.

Everything is in motion, Mera thought, smiling and thinking about how little of her life's motion she controlled. Her life was complicated, with many moving parts, and she hoped Havana would be a nice break from the pressure. She pushed herself up in her seat and leaned forward, looking directly below. It's so fragile and beautiful from the air. The Florida Keys were always on the edge of disaster with the constant threat of hurricanes. It's what made them so attractive, so alluring. It's that kind of thinking that makes your life so complicated, she thought, smiling to herself.

Having also spotted Key West, Phoebe had been thinking about Hemingway's connection to Key West and Cuba as the plane descended into Havana. For the last 10 minutes, their view had been the Gulf Stream and the deep, purple water that gave away its depth but not its mysteries.

"It doesn't seem possible," Phoebe said, leaning out into the narrow isle so Mera could hear her over the roar of the engines.

"What doesn't?" Mera asked.

"That we can live this close to Havana, Cuba, and yet it feels so far away."

The women chatted, unaware they had caught the eye of a dark-skinned Cuban. She was dressed entirely in white and wearing a turban-style headdress. She wore large, gold hoop earrings decorated with filigree and several gold bangle bracelets that made a jangling noise with the slightest movement of her wrist. Sitting in the aisle seat one row up, the woman turned to Mera and Phoebe and asked if this was their first time in Cuba.

"I have been here one time before," Phoebe said.

"It's my first time," Mera added.

The plane jolted as it turned left toward the runway on its continued descent.

"Well, welcome back and welcome the first time," the woman said in English with a thick Cuban accent. "My name is Caridad. What brings you to Cuba?" Caridad asked with a smile that revealed several gold teeth.

"We are here for the Hemingway Colloquium," Mera said.

"Yes, it's my first time presenting at a Hemingway conference," Phoebe added.

"Ah, Hemingway," Caridad said with a look of satisfaction. "Hemingway was a great believer in Cuban culture and spirituality."

"His story of Santiago has many references to the Afro-Cuban religions prevalent here on the island," Caridad said with a conspiratorial look.

Caridad's tone and expression struck Mera and Phoebe as strange and foreboding.

The plane jolted again as it descended through the low cloud cover, and the captain announced the imminent landing.

"I didn't know Hemingway had such a deep connection," Mera said. As Caridad started rummaging through her large cloth purse.

Even though she had read quite a bit about the religious and spiritual aspects of the story in preparation for the colloquium, the researchers had approached the work and the symbolism through the lens of a traditional, primarily Catholic perspective. She was excited at this opportunity to hear the perspective of a Cuban.

"Yes," Caridad said. "His custom was always to learn as much about his surroundings as possible. He was a great believer in knowing about the social and religious customs of the people he lived with. It was true in Paris and Spain when he wrote about bullfighting and the Spanish Civil War."

"Yes, that's true," Mera said. "He certainly had a way of describing not only landscapes and manmade surroundings but also the culture and temperament of the people he was writing about."

The plane touched down, and Mera and Phoebe stared at Caridad, intrigued by the small woman's take on Hemingway and his writing. Neither of them had expected to start their experience with a conversation about the author on the plane coming into Havana.

As they taxied to the terminal, Caridad found what she was looking for, pulling out two yellowish-green rings with a vert-de-gris patina. They were about an inch and a half across. Caridad looked at the two women and handed each of them a ring.

"I want you to have these," she said.

Phoebe and Mera studied the rings, turning them over in their hands. Caridad continued: "They were made by an ancient civilization that flourished in the region, now called Mali, many centuries ago."

"How did they end up in your possession?" Mera asked.

"They have been in my family for generations," Caridad said. "They came across the Atlantic with my ancestors, who were delivered to Regla as enslaved people. No one in my family knows how they smuggled them onto the island. Even without this knowledge, we have used them for sacred, religious rituals since our arrival. My great-grandmother claimed they had special powers, and I believed her. She was a powerful woman and talked to those on the other side. She also saw the future."

Caridad omitted the part about curing or seasoning the rings in her *Nganga*, which had taken many years. The gift of a relic from a *Nganalera* was unique and powerful, but she didn't want either of the two women to know how special and consequential it was.

"These are special to you," Phoebe said. She looked at the petite lady dressed in white and wondered why Caridad was trying to make a gift of these relics.

"Yes," Mera agreed. "I can't possibly take something so valuable to you and your family."

Caridad looked at the two women, thinking carefully about what to say next.

"I understand you are reluctant to accept this gift," Caridad said. "But the fact is, my family has been making gifts of these relics for almost five hundred years. Gifting to the right people was the primary purpose of bringing them across the ocean in the first place. When our ancestors arrived in Cuba from Nigeria, these were the only personal items they carried. The history of the people who made them is mostly lost to us. We know they came from the region of Guimbala in Mali, and they had a highly sophisticated and richly artistic metalworking tradition living along the inner Niger River Delta."

"If you don't mind my asking, how did you decide to give each of us one?" Phoebe asked. "You must have a small number left if your family has been giving them away for generations."

"Everyone in my family is blessed with the vision of our ancestors," Caridad said. "We are always aware of our surroundings, the people with whom we come in contact, and the energy they possess. Our family decided a long time ago to spread the energy of our ancestors to the people who can help us live out our destiny and, in turn, discover their own. It would be best to consider the rings a reminder of your search for your path and purpose. The rings will introduce you to the energy that vibrates at a higher frequency and remind you that you are both part of this energy. I feel we will meet again in Havana. If not, remember the story of the rings and keep their existence to yourselves."

The seatbelt sign turned off, and everyone on the plane, except for the three women, stood and started for the door.

"Are you here by yourselves?" Caridad asked.

"No, we are meeting two friends," Phoebe answered. "They are attending the conference as well."

"One is Cuban," Caridad said. It wasn't a question; it was a statement.

"Yes, one is Cuban," Mera said. "How in the world would you know?"

"It's an easy guess," Caridad said, smiling. "We are, after all, in Cuba now."

Phoebe and Mera exchanged puzzled glances.

Caridad hadn't made a guess; she had experienced a vision. She felt a familiar vibration when she handed the rings to Phoebe and Mera. She was convinced they had a connection to her dream and the son she was so desperate to meet.

"It's important you keep the rings with you in Havana," Caridad said as she gathered her things and stood. "They must be with you for the remainder of the trip. What you do with them after you leave Havana is up to you. You will discover why you have them and what you are supposed to do with them as part of your journey here on the island. The rings will help you."

Caridad stood and walked toward the door, the bangles on her wrist making a soft, trilling sound.

Phoebe and Mera looked at each other in silence. They grabbed their carry-ons and followed Caridad toward the exit.

Havana awaited, and the island's mystery was now front and center.

"This trip is starting with a bang," Mera said. "Is it always this exciting before you get off the plane?"

"No," Phoebe said. "This is a new one for me."

Jesús

After clearing customs, the health check ladies, and baggage claim, Mera and Phoebe are standing at the front of the airport amid the frenetic energy and motion of hundreds of people trying to find their way home.

"Wow," Mera said. "You were right. You can't imagine what this many 1950s-era cars look like until you see them all together like this."

"That's why I didn't try to explain," Phoebe said, smiling.

Phoebe spotted a driver waving as he turned to open the rear door of a dark green car.

"I think this is our ride," Phoebe said as she pointed to him.

"That one looks like fun!" Mera said. "And he looks like a nice guy. Let's take it."

"*Hola, como estas?*" Phoebe said, testing some of her Spanish.

"*Hola!*" the driver said. "*Estoy bien y tú?*"

"*Bien gracias,*" Mera answered. She looked at Phoebe, smiling. "I might as well get in the game, right?"

The driver loaded their bags into the trunk, and Phoebe caught a glimpse of his name tag. Ragged around the edges, it looked like it was printed before the revolution.

"His name is Jesús," Phoebe said. It seemed fitting as the encounter now seemed more like a rescue than a cab ride.

"We have an address of where we are going," Phoebe said to Jesús in English, hoping he understood. "The address is the corner of Avenida 23 and Calle E. The Elita Apartments."

"We have it written down," Mera said.

"Ah, that will be very good," Jesús said in broken but perfectly understandable English.

"Wonderful!" Phoebe said.

"Well, here it is." Mera handed him the paper.

"Ok," Jesús said. "You are staying in Vedado! That is a very nice neighborhood. I know right where it is."

"Our friend told us to ask the price before we leave," Phoebe said, smiling. She was trying not to insult Jesús, but Julian had been specific about not leaving in a taxi until they had established the fare.

"Yes, yes, yes!" Jesús said as he looked in his rear-view mirror at the woman. Both were smiling now; Mera having caught on to Phoebe's attempts at being charming and diplomatic.

Jesús thought they were a little too aggressive with the smiling, but he wanted them to be happy with the price. "40 CUCs," he said. "From here to Vedado, 40 CUC's. This is a fair price, I promise!"

This was a fair price; Julian had said it would be anywhere from 45 to 50 CUCs.

Still smiling too broadly, Phoebe said, "Ok, *¡gracias!*"

Maricel

Jesús loaded the luggage into the cavernous trunk as Caridad watched from a distance. He was taking good care of the women, and she knew he would deliver them to their destination. She also knew Jesús would report where they were staying and with whom.

As the car pulled away, Caridad's granddaughter, Maricel, walked up beside her.

"Did you have a good flight, Yayi?" She asked.

"Yes, I did," Caridad said. "I met those two lovely women. They were interested in our family story, and I was interested in hearing about their visit to Havana."

"Did you give them rings?" Maricel asked.

It was the question Maricel always asked when her grandmother said she had met someone.

"Yes," Caridad said, smiling. "They are here for the Hemingway Colloquium. They are meeting two friends who are also here for the Colloquium. Thank you for arranging for Jesús to take them to Havana."

"Of course," Maricel said. "It was lucky that he had driven me to meet you."

"Yes, lucky indeed," Caridad said.

"I thought you were trying to figure out where we were waiting for you," Maricel said.

Caridad was convinced the two women were connected to the son. She was convinced the son was in Cuba for more than the conference. Other than the fact he existed and was now here on the island, there were no further details. But the energy she felt with the two women on the plane was strong, and their connection to the son was unmistakable.

"I am sure these women are connected to the person in the dream," she said. "Hopefully, they will help us find him."

Caridad shared her dream with Maricel after it returned to her the first several nights. She shared everything with Maricel, and she knew she would need her granddaughter's help to find its meaning.

"I have no doubt," Maricel said. "You always choose wisely Yayi."

Caridad was still smiling as she watched Jesús' green Chevrolet pull away from the curb.

The Elita

We had been waiting at the entrance of the apartment building for some time when Mera and Phoebe arrived. Julian went to the curb and introduced himself to the driver. He and Jesús exchanged a few words. Both men laughed, and Julian paid him before Mera or Phoebe could reach for their purses.

"This one's on me," Julian said. "I wasn't sure if you had any CUCs."

"We appreciate it," Phoebe said. "We had some trouble with luggage at the airport and left without thinking about changing money."

"I had trouble," Mera said. "Phoebe's luggage was out in a few minutes. I was convinced mine was lost forever."

"Welcome to the Cuban pace!" Julian said, smiling. "We can't be rushed." He laughed and gestured to the women to start toward the apartment building we would call home for the next four days.

They turned to look at the 11-story building, the tallest on the block, painted in a burnt yellow hue with white and pink coral accents. Their temporary home boasted advantageous views in this residential neighborhood of mostly two-story homes. Like much of Havana, including their building, none were in good repair. Evidently, in the thirties, this was an upscale neighborhood. The large homes spoke of affluence. In slightly better repair than the surrounding houses, their apartment building featured a broad, sweeping staircase leading to the second-floor entrance.

We gathered their luggage and walked up the stairs. Emilio made a friendly gesture, and Julian introduced Phoebe and Mera as we entered the elevator.

"Are we sure this thing is safe?" Phoebe asked, looking at the ancient elevator.

"Of course not," Julian answered, smiling. "Why would we assume that?"

"Ok, just checking," Phoebe said, looking worried.

"Why do you think we took the 4th-floor apartment?" I asked. "Less of a jolt when we hit the ground."

"Very funny," Phoebe said.

"At least we get the top view," Mera said. "That should compensate for the added risk of hitting the ground from 11 stories up."

The ride up was uneventful, and as we exited the elevator, the landing and hallway were open air. Some other residents on the floor had decorated the outdoor space with plants in large clay pots of varying sizes.

"This is so tropical," Mera said. "Is the entire city like this?"

"Pretty much," I said. "You can tell you are in a different reality now, right?"

The two-bedroom apartment was a mix of mid-twentieth-century style and modern renovations—furnished with casual rattan and Cuban mahogany furniture. A faint blend of perfume, mango, and guava hung in the air. Mera spotted a collection of fresh fruit on the dining room table, recognizing large mangoes and smaller, yellowish guavas.

The walls were covered in prints and photographs of mostly religious iconography. The windows faced northwest, with a partial view to the east. The view was everything Mera and Phoebe could have hoped to have.

"Well, we'll let you ladies settle in," I said. "What's a good time to meet downstairs?"

"How about thirty minutes," Mera said. "That should give us enough time to unpack and freshen up. I'm anxious to see some of Havana."

"That works for me," Phoebe said.

"We will see you downstairs in thirty minutes, then," Julian said. "We are in apartment 4C, in case you need anything."

"You know you can't call us, right?" I said.

"Oh, right," Mera said. "It will take me a while to get used to the fact our phones don't work here. It certainly adds a layer of complexity to the adventure."

"Don't get lost," Phoebe said.

"Got it!" Mera said, smiling. She turned to Julian and me. "We will see you downstairs in thirty minutes."

Back in the apartment, Mera walked over to the large window at the end of the living room. She was facing north, with a view of the Gulf Stream as it reacted to the late afternoon light, giving the famous current its familiar deep purple color. Looking down at the streets and the buildings below, the rooftops reminded her of a Delacroix painting. The tropical blues and reds mixed with the vibrant greens gave the sultry afternoon a surreal look and feel.

Looking west, she noticed their apartment was next to a Catholic church whose steeple was finished in a baroque-style filigree. Painted yellow with white trim, it stood out on the street that was otherwise very residential. The Avenida 23 was six lanes of traffic and ran to the ocean looking east. The sun, arcing to the left, was hanging low over the Malecón, and the traffic on the street below was moving lazily in both directions.

Mera looked up and glanced north, knowing Key West was perched on the ancient coral ninety miles away. Even though she had seen it just a few hours ago, it felt so far away in both time and distance.

She remembered the story of seeing the Sand Key Lighthouse on a hot, humid night. Even though she knew it was impossible, she thought having such an appropriate experience would be fantastic, given Hemingway's frequent references to the Sand Key light in his writing.

Deep in thought and absent-minded wandering, Mera walked to the back of the apartment, where she found a small washer and dryer in a makeshift utility room.

"Hey Phoebe, there's a washing machine back here," she said. "It's small, but if we need to do some laundry, at least we have a machine."

"That's fantastic," Phoebe said. "I was wondering how I would make it in this heat."

The women went to their rooms and unpacked. Each room had its own air-conditioner, so the sleeping spaces were cool and comfortable even in the warm weather. The hum of the wall unit provided a soothing white noise that made the room private and intimate.

Unpacking quickly, Mera arranged the small bathroom with her supplies. Smiling at herself in the mirror, she marveled at being in Cuba. Eleven months ago, she thought Hemingway conferences and exotic travels were behind her, at least for a while. Yet, here she was, on a new adventure with close friends who understood her. Paris felt like a distant dream, but it happened, leaving an indelible mark on her feelings.

Havana was a mystery, and the unfolding would take place with her friends as an integral part of the experience. Just like Paris, where possibilities were endless, Havana held a similar promise for Mera. She was sure the two cities were connected beyond Hemingway. Havana, the Paris of the Caribbean, she reminded herself. The glimpses of architecture she caught were incredible, and she knew there was much more to explore. Time would be too short, but she vowed to make the most of it with the city and her friends. Julian was the key. This was his home; he looked genuinely alive here, and he and Max seemed closer than ever.

Phoebe knocked on the bedroom door.

"Mera, are you ready?"

"Yes, I'll be out in a minute."

Mera took one last look in the mirror. She hadn't seen a reflection looking back so vibrant and excited since Paris.

She reached into her purse and felt for the ring Caridad had given her, running her fingers around the outside and feeling the roughness of the surface. Now, she was ready. She opened the door and smiled at Phoebe.

"Do you have your ring?" She asked.

"Absolutely," Phoebe answered, holding it up on her index finger like jewelry.

"Off we go then," Mera said.

Havana was waiting. It was time to see what the city had in store for the next four days.

Old Havana

Julian hailed a taxi and asked the driver to take the tour around the Malecón. As always, he was sitting in the front, and I was sitting in the back with Mera and Phoebe.

"*¿Cómo te llamas*, Amigo?" Julian asked the driver his name.

"*Mi nombre es Renaldo*," the driver said.

"*Cubano?*" Renaldo asked.

"*Si*," Julian answered. "Yes, I am Cuban."

And so, the conversation in the front seat was off and running, with Julian gathering intel and the three of us in the back taking in the sights.

The sea had calmed since Phoebe and Mera had driven by earlier. As the taxi made its way east, the sun was beginning to set at our backs, and soon, the last of the day's light would be bathing the façades of the buildings in amber. The changing light and shadows were already changing the mood of the famous boulevard.

The taxi continued slowly along the broad avenue, past the traffic circle, and up to and past the Hotel Nacional with its imposing rock wall. The ocean was quiet, and the view of El Morro was spectacular in the fading light as it grew closer.

"It's so beautiful," Mera said as we rode along the boulevard, taking in the sights and sounds of the island's most famous drive.

"The Malecón is arguably the most recognized part of Havana," Julian said.

The mist was coming up over the seawall, even without a heavy sea. It gave a sense of intrigue to the island, and Mera was getting her first taste of the allure and mystery Havana always evoked.

As Renaldo made the sweeping right turn at the mouth of Havana Harbor, El Morro was in complete and splendid view.

"Wow," Mera said. "What an amazing sight. What an amazing place."

"This is what started it all," I said. "If it weren't for this harbor, Havana wouldn't exist. And Cuba might have been left alone for another one or two hundred years."

"Columbus fell in love with Cuba the moment he saw it, and before he knew there was a deep-water harbor," Julian said. "When he landed at Baracoa, he encountered the Taíno and found them quite friendly and accommodating."

Julian directed Renaldo to the Plaza de Armas between the fort and the Hotel Santa Isabel. A small taxi stand offered safety from the waterfront traffic.

He settled up with Renaldo, and we climbed out of the car and onto the sidewalk. As we stepped out, three older gentlemen crowded around Phoebe and Mera. Two were holding guitars, and one was holding maracas.

"Oh, Jesus!" I said, smiling and backing away because I wanted Phoebe and Mera to have the whole experience.

Sure enough, the lead musician started the festivities with some banter.

"*Hola*, lovely ladies! What a beautiful evening, and what beautiful ladies! We have a beautiful song for you and will play it now."

Mera was smiling, and Phoebe looked a little skeptical, but she was taking her cue from me, smiling and encouraging the three gentlemen.

Julian came around the taxi as the three musicians broke into a spirited version of "Hotel California." It continued for some time, and combining the guitars and the maracas lent a unique interpretation and mood to the Eagles' classic. All three elderly gentlemen were quite good, and Phoebe and Mera were thoroughly entertained. When the music stopped, everyone was pleased.

"Wow," Phoebe said. "These guys are something."

"They are," I said. "We know them. They are always here in front of the old fort."

"Why "Hotel California"?" Mera asked. "It's an odd choice of songs."

"Almost all of the street bands play it," I said. "I have this running debate with Julian about why it's so popular. He says it's because they all think it will be popular with American tourists. I say it's a hidden cry for help. You know, references to being prisoners, checking out but never leaving—all those things."

Julian approached the oldest of the musicians and hugged him.

"Amigo, how have you been," Julian asked in English.

"Ah, I have been feeling not so good, Amigo," the oldest gentleman said.

"I'm sorry to hear that," Julian replied. "Here is something for you and your wife." Julian handed the man several CUC bills. "Please tell her I said hello."

"I will tell her I saw you," the old man said. "She will be pleased. Are you here long?"

"We are all here for a few days," Julian said. "We are attending a Hemingway Conference over at the Riviera. Perhaps I will see you and Magdalena before I leave."

"That would be nice," the old man said. "We would enjoy playing again for the ladies."

"*Son Hermosos*—they're beautiful," the old man said in Spanish with a mischievous smile.

"*Son amigos*—they're friends," Julian said, smiling back. "Next time, you can play some Cuban music. I think they would like that."

"It will be our pleasure," the old man said.

Julian passed some CUCs to the other two gentlemen. They looked at him and thanked him, holding their hands together as if praying.

"*Mucho gracias*," they said. One touched Julian's arm.

Julian smiled. "*Ashé, Amigos*," he said.

They smiled and bowed their heads before moving on to the next taxi and the next iteration of "Hotel California."

Julian started across the Plaza in front of El Templete, crossing in front of the Santa Isabel to Obispo, taking a left at Oficios Street, and walking toward the Plaza de San Francisco. Many shops were still open, and it was Mera's first look at Old Havana at dusk. He led the group down Oficios Street, turning left onto Tenienté and crossing over Mercadéres at the corner of Plaza Vieja.

Mera stopped at the corner of Mercadéres and Teniente to take in the narrow street's details, a classic Havana scene. Tall buildings with balconies serving various purposes—some draped with laundry like United Nations flags, others set for imagined romantic dinners. Small children lined up on some, watching the foot traffic below. Some balconies hosted women sharing gossip and men smoking cigars as they called out to flamboyant strollers. Flirting and the dance of social interaction were the affordable, inclusive pastimes that animated the street.

She was lost in the exchange between a young Cuban couple when she heard Julian calling to her.

"Let's go, straggler!"

She smiled, remembering why she liked traveling with her friends. She hurried to catch up, and as she did, she realized they were at the restaurant. Julian had gone ahead and was already talking to a nice-looking young man standing at the entrance.

Cheers

Café Mercaderes, a walk-up restaurant on the second floor overlooking the street, welcomed diners with a narrow staircase adorned with rose petals and votive candles. The walls flanking the stairwell showcased rescued objects turned into eclectic wall art—oil paintings framed and unframed, mingling with photographs in varying conditions. The mix included household items and everyday tools, once used in kitchens around Havana for mundane and exotic tasks, dating from the turn of the century until the 1960s, the time of the revolution.

The room buzzed at the top of the stairs with an intense mix of sights, sounds, and smells. A diverse clientele, locals and tourists, fueled loud and raucous conversations in Spanish, English, French, and German. A band squeezed onto a tiny balcony, playing music that complimented the lively discussions. Nearly all tables were occupied, the kitchen was in full swing, and the enticing smell of food filled the air. We had heard good things about the restaurant, creating high anticipation for Phoebe and Mera. We were all eager for the experience.

Julian negotiated a prime table overlooking the street. The waiter showed up with water, and before long, a round of mojitos was on the table. They went down quickly with the anticipation of dinner, motivating a quick end to the cold, refreshing liquid.

Next came a plate of grilled grouper on plantains with a remoulade sauce. Julian ordered an Albariño, and the waiter opened the bottle and let Phoebe have a taste. She nodded her approval, and the waiter poured the wine around the table.

"Julian, this is amazing," Mera said. She looked up and down Mercaderes and watched the people strolling along the street.

"I'm glad you like it," Julian said, smiling.

"To Mera's first night," I said, reaching across the table to touch glasses.

"To Mera," Julian and Phoebe said.

Mera tasted the wine. It was cold and citrusy. It reminded her of a Chardonnay, not the oaky California style but the French style with no oak and a flinty, mineral finish. She liked how it made her feel. It reminded her of Paris.

"This is a beautiful space," Phoebe said. "I wonder who decorated the walls. I love the vision."

"The artwork and all the items are from the early 20th century," I said. "It's typical for restaurants in Havana to have this motif."

"I love all of the old china and silverware," Mera said. "It's all so retro."

"There's a reason for that," I said, looking at Mera. "But before we get into that, it's time for you to earn your dinner."

The waiter returned, and it was time to order.

"This wine calls for seafood, don't you think?" I said.

"Definitely," Mera said.

"Fish or shellfish?" Phoebe asked.

"Let's see if they have any specials," I said.

Julian asked the waiter if there was anything not on the menu.

"*Si*," the waiter said. "We have black marlin tonight. It is fresh off the docks this afternoon. The chef prepares it grilled with an olive oil drizzle and some fresh vegetables."

"How is it?" I asked.

"It is excellent," the waiter said.

"I have never had black marlin," Phoebe said. "I am anxious to try it."

Phoebe placed her order, and everyone else followed her lead and ordered the marlin. Once the waiter left, all eyes turned to Mera.

"So, how's it going so far?" I asked, smiling.

"There isn't any way to describe, much less understand, what I've seen since landing at Jose Martí Airport this morning. It's impossible to take it all in. I can't reconcile the suffering with the beauty. Why do I feel so guilty about how beautiful the island is and how beautiful the people are? Julian, your family has been through so much. I have no sense of how serious their struggle is."

Julian looked at her with a mixture of understanding and sympathy. She was right. He had heard this reaction many times before. Every time he returned to Cuba, he struggled with his conflicted feelings. His family's struggles were very real. He did what he could to help them, but only so much could be done. They live in the reality of the social and economic dynamic that the government and the embargo dictate.

"What must the Cuban people think of us?" Mera asked. "We have caused them so much pain and suffering with the embargo."

The food arrived as if on cue. The fish was cooked to perfection. As with most of the meals in Havana, everything was fresh. The table went quiet as everyone concentrated on eating.

After their meal, the waiter delivered four shot glasses and a bottle of Havana Club Reserva rum. Julian was smiling as Mera looked at the bottle and the glasses confusedly.

"Welcome to another Havana tradition," Julian said. This is how we end every meal. Of course, sometimes it's with rum and a cigar, but this restaurant only provides the rum."

"When I think I can't find anything else to like about Havana," Mera said with a mischievous smile.

"I can assure you; this won't be the last of it either," Phoebe said, looking at Mera with a conspiratorial grin and a wink.

The waiter poured the shots of dark rum, and Julian did the honors.

"To Mera's first night in Havana. May there be many more. And may the *Orisha* who chooses her be wise and kind and guide her through her journey of discovery."

The dinner had been light and celebratory. So much had been packed into such a long day that it was hard not to feel exhilarated and exhausted. Havana's history and charm were working their magic. It was a dynamic I had seen play out many times. Even Phoebe, who had been to the island, was not immune to its charms.

Julian's shift in mood during the toast was not lost on me. His mention of the *Orishas* and the toast to Mera had been made in all seriousness. Julian was subtle by nature, so it was easy to miss.

I looked at Mera and Phoebe. They were holding their glasses at the ready. Julian maintained eye contact with Mera, and she was smiling. He wasn't smiling, but I didn't think Mera noticed. She looked radiant and relaxed but didn't see the moment like I did.

The room became still, and as if on cue, the band stopped playing. I felt the slight vibration, and there was a small, almost imperceptible shift of light in the room.

"*Ashé*," Julian said, moving his shot glass toward the center of the table.

I looked at Julian and knew there would be more to come, a reckoning or more like a reconciliation.

"*Ashé*," Mera and Phoebe said, touching their glasses to mine and Julian's. They were still smiling. The restaurant was mostly empty, and the silence continued. The band was starting to pack up.

"*Ashé*," I said, looking at my three friends.

The shot glasses touched. Julian took a sip and then downed the glass of rum, letting the warmth fill his mouth and run down his throat. We all followed his lead.

It was Julian's way of resetting the mood before Mera or Phoebe noticed the seriousness of his demeanor.

"Wow, that was intense," Phoebe said. "Why the hell did we do that?"

"Drank it like vodka!" Mera said. "I liked it!"

The waiter came to the table with a food container and handed it to Julian. Everyone chipped in for the tab. Julian grabbed the food as they all stood and headed for the door.

"Late-night snack?" Mera asked, looking at Julian holding the food.

"You'll see," I answered.

"You guys are full of surprises," Mera said.

Crossing the room, I led the way down the stairs and onto Mercaderes Street.

"Do you want to go back towards Plaza de Armas or to San Francisco?" I asked Julian.

"We can catch a cab in front of the San Francisco Plaza," Julian said.

Hector

We turned left toward Plaza de San Francisco at the restaurant's entrance. As usual, the music and drums were pulsing in the background. At the Plaza, Julian spotted an old man sitting on one of the benches in front of the stock exchange building. He walked over and started talking to him. I motioned Phoebe and Mera to continue toward the harbor where we would find the waiting taxis.

"What's he doing?" Mera asked.

"He never leaves a restaurant in Havana or anywhere in Cuba without food," Phoebe said. "Most of the time, it's leftover food from the meal, but if there aren't any leftovers, he orders extra food and has it boxed up. Then he finds someone on the street to give it to. He says he can always tell who's deserving by looking at them and talking to them."

"I don't doubt that," Mera said.

She looked back to see Julian talking to the old gentleman. She loved watching him talk to people in a crowd or one-on-one. There was always a level of intensity in the conversation with Julian when observed from a distance; this was no different. The scene was surreal, with the sound of the bongos and the claves setting the tempo. The old man was hunched over, listening to Julian.

"*Hola, Amigo,*" Julian said. "Such a beautiful evening, yes?"

"*Hola, Amigo,*" the old man replied. "Yes, a beautiful evening, to be sure."

"What is your name?" Julian asked.

"Hector," the old man replied.

"Hector, I don't want to insult you, but I have come from dinner and have some food I could not finish. Perhaps you or your family would like it?"

"You are too kind, Amigo," Hector said. "Under normal circumstances, I would be too proud to accept your offer, but my wife has been released from the hospital today, and we are staying here with family. We are already too much burden for them, so I will accept your offer."

"I am sorry to hear about your wife," Julian said. "I spoke to a good friend earlier today, and his wife was also having health issues. It saddens me when I hear of these things. I will say a prayer for your wife. What is her name?"

"Her name is Isabella. She will appreciate that very much, Amigo. Especially from someone of your importance."

"I am happy to do it, Hector. Please tell Isabella I will be thinking about her, and I hope this food will bring the two of you some comfort."

"This means a lot to us, Amigo. You have no idea how much this means to us. Since we have been in Havana, I have been trying to find work. No one wants to hire an old man."

"Hector, you are a good husband," Julian said. "Your wife is lucky to have you, and you are lucky to have her."

"It is true that I am lucky to have her," Hector said, smiling. "Her luck at having me is a question for further debate."

"Take care of yourself, Hector. Your wife needs you."

"I will. But I didn't get your name. What is your name?" Hector asked.

"My name is Julian."

"Thank you, Julian, you are a godsend. I don't know why you are in the Plaza or Havana, but I wish you great success in whatever you are trying to do."

"Thank you, Hector. You don't know how much that means to me."

Julian smiled and placed his hand on the old man's shoulder. There was nothing else to do, and he was sad he couldn't be of more help.

Mera watched Julian hand the food to the old man and gently touch him on the shoulder. She could see the old man straighten as Julian reached out. There was a moment when she thought the two of them would embrace, but the moment passed, and Julian said one last thing to him. Mera saw the old man smile. It was an ancient smile with melancholy and longing, and something about it made her feel she had witnessed something more intimate than it should have been. Julian paused momentarily, and Mera saw his energy pass briefly to the old man. Then he straightened, turned, walked toward them, and was himself again.

As Julian turned, he caught Mera's expression and knew she understood what had happened. He walked toward her, smiling as he came across the Plaza de San Francisco, made famous by Hemingway in the opening of *To Have and Have Not*. "You know how it is there . . . ," Harry Morgan says as he draws the reader into the reality of life in depression era Havana in 1935. Mera knows she is standing in the plaza where the bums hung out, and the ice man came, and the young Cuban revolutionaries risked their lives and lived and died in violent shootouts. The fiction came so close to the truth that no one knew what was true and what was made up. The famous Walker Evans took pictures of it in black and white, and the photographs were left with Hemingway in safekeeping, the images used as inspiration to create the dark and dangerous world of the protagonist.

Mera turned and walked toward the boulevard, toward me and Phoebe, with all the day's events and all the day's emotions swirling in her head and not ready to sort themselves out because she knew she was too tired and too weak to do it in any way that made sense. *Keep walking,* she thought. *It's the only thing keeping you from insanity at this moment.* Julian was behind her, but talking to him now would not help. There was too much to sort out, too much rum, too much emotion, and too little energy. As she walked, she could feel the ancient ballast stones, carried from New England and traded for rum and sugar cane, beneath her; they struck the bottoms of her feet and vibrated. It was an odd sensation, and she didn't know what to make of it. But the drums and the claves knew as they kept time with her footsteps. The vert-de-gris ring knew too.

As the vibration moved up into her pelvis and abdomen, there was a word to describe her feeling. Julian sensed what was happening to her and knew to give it space. He slowed so she could feel the full effect of the moment.

Mera was having trouble naming her experience. She knew there was a word, a fine word, that perfectly summed up what was happening. It would be many months before she could look back on that evening and that moment and know what the word was and why it was so perfect. At that moment of revelation, the *Duende* would be as real as it was that night in Havana, and it would finally have a name.

Julian caught up with them as they reached the Malecón.

"Did you find your deserving recipient?" I asked.

"I did, Amigo," Julian answered. "His name is Hector, and he was about to leave and go home to his wife. She was released from the hospital, and they are trying to return to Camagüey. He was trying to pick up odd jobs in the Plaza but was unsuccessful. They are staying with family outside Havana, but there is no room for them, and their family cannot afford to feed them any longer. He thanked me for the food and said he was grateful not to be a burden to his family tonight."

Julian walked to the edge of the boulevard and found a bright red '57 Chevrolet Impala. After a brief negotiation, he waved at us to climb in.

"Who wants a ride?" he asked.

"We all do," Phoebe said.

As usual, I climbed into the back with Phoebe and Mera, and Julian sat in the front. The exchange was made, and off we went. The driver, Vincento, made a U-turn and headed back toward the entrance to Havana Harbor.

There was no conversation, only the low roar of the Subaru diesel engine, which had replaced the Chevrolet standard, in-line, 6-cylinder engine years ago.

I wondered if the faint smell of diesel in the back seat had become familiar in the short time Phoebe and Mera had been on the island. The wind rushing by the slightly opened windows was now a welcomed sound for me, as the wind and the smell of the salt air mixed with the fumes, and made the whole experience real in ways the visual panorama couldn't.

I noticed Julian was not his usual chatty self, preferring to be lost in his thoughts. Vincento made the slow turn to the west with El Morro on the right and the new Prado Hotel on the left. The tide was high, and the wind was up. The Gulf Stream must have been close to shore because the waves were crashing against the sea wall, causing spray to come across the first two lanes of traffic. Vincento commented on the water in English, and Julian answered. Mera couldn't hear the exchange and leaned up to ask Julian what he said.

"He said he's glad the car is built like a tank with all this salt spray coming across the road."

The Hotel Nacional appeared, rising above the Malecón and looking as imposing as ever. Vincento turned left onto Avenida 23 and headed toward the apartments. The first day in Havana was about to close. It was late, and everyone was tired. Casa

Elita was rising on the right, and the Impala slowed, stopping at the curb where Avenida 23 crossed Calle E. I handed Julian 15 CUCs, and he paid Vincento.

"Gracias, Amigo," Julian said, patting his new friend on the shoulder. "Take good care of yourself."

"You too," Vincento replied. "You and your friends have a good time in Havana."

The four of us exited the car and headed up the steps.

City of Light

Mera was back in her room, ready for bed. It had been a long, eventful day with so many emotions and so much to see. The experience at the restaurant and the Plaza had given her a lot to think about, and the loneliness that was so familiar and so relentless was starting to get the upper hand. She stood in front of the window with the lights out and the curtain open as the air-conditioner battled the heat and humidity. The room, a blend of dark mahogany furniture, pine walls, and terrazzo flooring, was filled with the unmistakable scent of the 1950s. Walls seasoned with cigar smoke and Cuban cooking felt like a memorial to the spirit of the people.

The church steeple was prominent in the foreground, and the city stretched northward to the Malecón and then out to sea. She stood for a moment, trying to see the glow of the Sand Key lighthouse. She knew it wasn't possible, but she wanted it to be there to ease her sense of isolation.

She slipped into bed, thinking about Paris. The air-conditioner was humming; the sound made her think about the traffic on the street by the café, the taste of the wine, and how the nights had ended. She closed her eyes, imagining herself back in her room in Paris. It wasn't how she wanted to ease the loneliness, but it would have to do for now.

Caridad

In Guanabacoa, Caridad tended her altar, lighting a candle and praying to the Virgin of Regla and Atabey. She had given rings to the two Americans, hoping to make a connection to the person she was sure was the son in her dream. Jesús told her about the mulatto priest Julian, who paid the taxi fare from the airport. He fit the description, and she wanted to know more about him. She arranged for Jesús to be available for transportation, hoping Julian and Jesús would become friends.

Once Caridad knew where the women were staying, she reached out to the apartment's owner and arranged for Maricel to be the maid and cook for Phoebe and Mera. In any other circumstance, the fact Caridad knew the owner might be considered a coincidence, but Caridad didn't believe in coincidences, so the idea she could make the arrangement so quickly only increased her desire to know who Mera and Phoebe were traveling with and what their relationship was to the priest.

Between Jesús and Maricel, Caridad was confident she would discover where this journey led her. Whatever the path, she was sure there was a connection between the two women and the priest. The connection was strong with them, and the urge to give them the rings was the strongest she could remember in a long time.

Caridad summoned the energy of the totems she had carefully placed on her altar. The candles were casting the faintest of light on the crocheted cloth covering and the two ceramic tureens she had arranged amongst the other items. Both tureens contained sacred objects she had collected over the years. But the white tureen, with a simple green band around the lip, held her most cherished possessions. In addition to the sacred stones and small pieces of bone, this tureen held the last ring that matched the rings she had given to Phoebe and Mera. Using them to connect her to the unknown priest, she hoped they were doing the bidding she intended. There was an element of danger in what she was asking. While the Virgin could be forgiving, Atabey was not, and she would not be pleased if she were being summoned for petty matters.

She was now silent, meditating, and focused on listening to her heart and the message her ancestors and the *Orishas* might want her to hear. Her patron, Oshún, had been silent for too long, and Caridad hoped there would be a sign. She kneeled patiently. She knew these things could not be rushed, and there was plenty of time. The spirits would work at their own pace. The answers would come when they were ready.

"Poco a poco llega lejo," Caridad thought to herself—"Even with little steps, you can go far." It was an excellent thought to keep.

TUESDAY

Julio

The Cubans organized the first day of the conference with an unmistakable pacing and flavor. Presentations ranged from interpretations of *The Old Man and the Sea* to the meaning of religious iconography in Hemingway's writings from his earliest works until his latest posthumously published stories. Much of the discourse was esoteric and precise to the point of being almost opaque.

Gathered in the lobby after the last presentation, we were looking for a way to gracefully bow out of the groups forming dinner plans later in the evening. We planned to dine in Old Havana, explore Obispo Street, and enjoy the sights around the plazas.

"We should check on Julio one last time," Phoebe said, smiling.

Julio was the name Phoebe and Mera had given to the handsome bartender in the lobby bar at the Riviera Hotel.

"I don't think his name is Julio," I said. "And I'm quite sure he's left for the day. He doesn't work twenty-four hours a day waiting for the two of you."

"Are you sure?" Mera asked, feigning disappointment. "Maybe he knows we're still here, and he asked to work some overtime."

"Julian, can we put these two out of their misery and get a cab back to the apartments?" I asked.

"Absolutely," Julian said, smiling.

"Let's be clear," Phoebe said. "Checking on Julio doesn't make us miserable. It's the opposite. The guy is gorgeous, and ordering mojitos from him is the highlight of the conference."

"Julian?" I pleaded.

"Yes, Max," Julian replied, with a pained look as he walked toward the entrance looking to hail a cab.

"Come on, you two," I said. "Don't you want to see Old Havana? There's plenty more eye candy in the old city."

"Who's looking for eye candy," Phoebe said. "This isn't a spectator sport as far as I'm concerned."

We climbed into a 1954 Ford Fairlane with Julian in the front seat.

"*Buenas tardes, Amigo, nos dirigimos a nuestro apartamento en avenida 23 y calle E. Los Apartamentos Elita. ¿Cuánto llevarnos allí, por favor?*" Julian asked the driver the fare to return them to their apartment.

"*Buenas tardes, Amigo, te cobraré 15 CUCs porque eres un hermano, ¡un cubano!*" the driver said. "15 CUCs is the fare because you are a brother, a Cuban!"

"*Realmente aprecio eso, Amigo,*" I appreciate that, Julian said. "*Por favor, conduzca.*"

So, with the usual banter and negotiations, we were on our way back to the apartments.

"The weather looks threatening," Mera said as we pulled away from the Hotel.

"Yes, I think there might be storms later," Julian said.

"Wherever we go later, we might want to end up close to the Plaza de Armas for dinner," I said. "Julian, what about the restaurant in front of the Santa Isabel?"

"You're thinking of El Templete Marinero, Max," Julian said. "That's a good idea. If the weather turns bad, we will be close to the taxi stand and can return to the apartment without too much trouble. It's a lovely place, the food is good, and they have a nice wine selection and a full bar."

"It's also on the waterfront with a view of El Morro and Regla across the harbor," I said.

"You had me at full bar," Mera said, smiling.

"Me too!" Phoebe agreed.

Emilio was waiting for us with a big smile when we got to the Elita.

"Hola amigos and amigas!" he said.

Phoebe and Mera said hello as they caught the elevator upstairs to get ready. Julian waved them on.

"We will see you in a little while," I said. The women nodded in agreement and disappeared behind the closing doors.

Emilio motioned to Julian. *"Oyé,* Julian. Jesús came by a little while ago and said he was looking for you. He said you asked him about a ride later into Old Havana?"

"Si, Amigo. Did he say he was coming back?"

"Si. He said he would be back around 6:30. This is when you asked him to return."

"Si, si," Julian said. *"Perfecto.* Thank you, *Amigo."*

With arrangements made, we headed to the fourth floor to get ready for the evening.

On the 11th floor, when Phoebe walked out of her bedroom, Mera was looking out the window facing toward the harbor.

"Something's not right," Mera said, staring out the window.

"What?" Phoebe asked.

"With Julian, something isn't right. Have you noticed?" Mera asked.

"No," Phoebe said. "I think he's quiet but might be nervous about the film. Max is a little subdued, too. I thought they were thinking about the presentation tomorrow."

"I hope you're right," Mera said, looking worried. "I think . . . ," Mera didn't finish her thought.

"Maybe you should ask," Phoebe said.

"I don't know," Mera said. "I don't want to hover."

"It's time to go," Phoebe said. "The guys will be waiting for us downstairs."

When Phoebe and Mera arrived downstairs, they were surprised to see Jesús waiting for them.

"Jesús! What are you doing here?" Mera asked.

"I have come to take you downtown. *Mi Amigo,* Julian, asked if I could provide transportation while you were in town."

"Well, this is exciting! We are happy to see you," Phoebe said.

"And I am so happy to see you ladies also," Jesús said.

"Did you and Julian know each other before you brought us from the airport?" Mera asked. "That would be quite the coincidence."

"No, he and I met yesterday," Jesús said. "I think it's a good idea to plan ahead. Don't you?"

"Absolutely!" Mera answered. "I'm always amazed at how quickly Julian makes friends."

Thunder and Lightning

The sky was heavy with dark clouds when we reached the Plaza, and the wind intensified. Julian suggested we head to the restaurant for drinks and an early dinner to wait out the rain.

"Sounds like a great plan," Phoebe said.

"I agree," Mera added.

Walking from the foot of O'Reilly Street, we turned left at the corner of El Templete, the first of many churches built in Havana. We continued across the plaza in front of Santa Isabel and headed toward the narrow alley leading to the restaurant entrance.

As we turned onto the plaza, the drums played Afro-Cuban and Abakuá rhythms, and claves filled the air. Phoebe and Mera paused, absorbing the ambiance that would become this trip's indelible memory. Stopping momentarily to listen, they looked at each other and Julian.

He seemed most at home in this place, the oldest part of Havana. The Spaniards, the English, the French, and the Portuguese had all landed here. All of the invaders arrived under the watchful eye of the Ceiba tree. Each planted their flags as if they could truly own the island.

Standing on the remnants of New England ballast stones, now paving the plaza, Mera and Phoebe remembered the human ballast from Africa that had landed at Regla as fodder for the fields and farms. They remembered hearing about the first time the Taíno met the Spaniards and the ravages of the violence and disease that followed. They remembered meeting Caridad on the plane, and without speaking, they clutched the rings she had given them.

I had walked ahead, but Julian, sensing the electricity in the air from the storm, stopped and turned to look at Mera and Phoebe. He knew they were in the city's thrall, and he waited until they had seen what they wanted to see and felt what they needed to feel. Walking over slowly, he stood next to them. They hadn't seen or heard him coming, the drums and the claves having supplied the cover of his movement.

They knew they should have been startled by his sudden presence, but instead, it seemed natural that he was standing next to them. They felt the electricity, too.

"We should go before the rain starts," Julian said.

There was a faint flash of lightning to the north as if on cue, and the first of the thunder, a low rumbling, sounded in the distance.

"Yes," Phoebe and Mera said in unison. The women looked back at the plaza and toward Obispo Street. The sounds of the drums and claves were softer, and the light was more delicate, too. Julian had walked on ahead to catch up with me. Mera and Phoebe followed. No one spoke until we reached the restaurant.

Sitting across the harbor in Guanabacoa, Caridad lit a candle and said a prayer. It was more of a promise to Atabey, and the energy coursing through her body gave her a hint of the changes that were about to come. She had suspected there was a new destiny for her and her family. She felt it for the first time when she met the two women on the plane. She knew they weren't the answer, but she was convinced they would lead her to the answer. She knew they would lead her to who she was looking for.

The Temple

El Templete Marinero, behind and to the right of the Santa Isabel hotel, offered views of Havana harbor and Regla.

Phoebe suggested wine to start. The thunder was getting louder as the waiter arrived with our selection. Wine in Havana is limited, but Phoebe had chosen a Chilean Cabernet with excellent structure and depth.

I looked over at Julian, who was smiling.

"Ok, what's with the big grin?" I asked.

"Nothing," Julian responded. "It's been a while since I experienced a storm this intense in the old city."

"It reminds me of the storm at Aunt Nita's house a couple of years ago," I said. "That was a magical evening, and now I always think of it when we're in a storm here on the island."

"I have that same reaction," Julian said.

As we sipped the wine, the weather intensified. The wind, coming in gusts, was buffeting the rain. Combined with the thunder and lightning, it was putting on quite a show.

It wasn't long before our food arrived—fresh shrimp, fish, and a second bottle of wine. Soon, everyone was enjoying dinner while nature entertained. The Dorado and shrimp were cooked in a hearty tomato sauce seasoned with garlic, citrus, and a combination of spices that stood up well to the Cabernet.

Julian was staring at Phoebe and Mera. Both women were looking out across the boulevard and toward Regla. The look in their eyes was familiar as the city's rhythm entered their psyche.

He knew the seduction was inevitable. They would soon be in love with the island. While it was never a foregone conclusion, he would do his best to ensure it happened.

"What's going on in that head of yours, Amigo?" I asked.

Julian smiled.

"It's time to go to Regla," Julian said. "Phoebe and Mera won't understand Cuba without visiting and understanding those places. Tomorrow, we will go to Regla, and they can hear and see the island's history from the perspective of the people who worship the Virgin."

Julian looked relieved to say what he was thinking; that was how it appeared to me. In truth, he was relieved to finally be on his way.

WEDNESDAY

Maricel

Maricel Arango Sosa is 18 years old and can't remember a time before she considered herself a dancer. She also can't remember a time before being dedicated to mastering the ancient Palo and Taíno rituals. From the moment she started walking, Caridad told her she would be chosen to carry on the traditions of the Palo religion and the most sacred and powerful chants. Maricel's demeanor exudes quiet confidence, and her movements are deliberate as if every step is a dance step. To anyone familiar with the physical traits of a dancer, she moves with the unmistakable confidence and balance that belie her years of intense training. There's a serenity about her, an aura of wisdom beyond her years, as she carries the weight of generations in her purposeful pursuit of preserving and performing these sacred practices.

"He will be there this morning," the voice said. Maricel couldn't tell if the voice was the Virgin of Regla or her grandmother. She often had trouble distinguishing between the two in her dreams.

"He will be there this morning, and I want you to ask him about his intentions," the Virgin, or her grandmother, said.

Maricel was confused because the woman was not dressed as her grandmother but in the flowing blue dress of the Virgin. Maricel loved her grandmother and dreamt of her often. At an early age, Caridad told Maricel that she had the "gift," and it would be up to her to use it. Initially, she had been frightened about it but accepted it over the years. She knew her grandmother also had the "gift," and this gave Maricel a powerful connection to her.

"When you see him, ask him about his father. Make sure he tells you about his father," the woman dressed as the Virgin said.

In the fog of her dream, Maricel decided it was her grandmother because Caridad had arranged to get her the job of preparing and serving breakfast to the two women staying at the apartment in Vedado. It didn't make any sense that the virgin would be interested in this man's comings and goings.

When she heard the rooster, Maricel was already awake. She heard someone in the small kitchen on the other side of the thin door, and she knew it was her mother, her aunt, or both, making coffee and whatever meager breakfast they could come up with for the morning.

Laying on the small cot she shared with her cousins, Maricel thought it was either her mother or her aunt; if it were both, they would talk to each other as if it were the middle of the day. After a few minutes, the smell of coffee drifted into the room, and the sounds of movement in the family room were more pronounced. Now, her parents', aunts', and uncles' voices filled the room as they prepared for the day.

The routine never changed. Parents first made breakfast and prepared for work, taking turns using the single bathroom. Then, children were called, usually in age order. Maricel, the oldest and working in Vedado, won the priority on two counts and got the next bathroom turn. Responding to a slight knock on the door, she gathered her morning essentials and slipped quietly from the bedroom, kissing each of her parents on the way to the bathroom.

She glanced out the open double door leading to a tiny balcony overlooking the two-lane street in front of their building. Even though the sun had barely breached the horizon, cars, trucks, and people were moving about, and the city's energy was already ramping up.

You learn to get ready efficiently when you share one bathroom with ten other people. Maricel was no exception, and in a matter of a few minutes, she was bathed and dressed, having applied all the makeup she could afford, and her hair styled to her satisfaction.

When she emerged from the bathroom, her father had already left for his job at the road department, and her mother was about to leave.

"I'm leaving, Maricel," her mother said. "Please be careful going to Vedado."

"I will, Mama," Maricel answered. "This is not my first job in Vedado, you know."

"I know, Maricel, but you know I can't stand that ferry across the harbor from Regla. That harbor is full of sharks."

"I know, Mama, but the weather is good, and it is early. If the weather is bad later, I promise I won't take it to come home."

Maricel's commute involves a bike ride to the Regla ferry, the ferry ride, a bus trip to Vedado, and a walk to the apartment building where the two women are staying. She had never seen sharks in the harbor between Regla and the landing in old Havana, but she knew it wouldn't do any good to tell her mother such a thing.

"I wish Yayí hadn't gotten you this job. It's too far away, and it's too hard to get to."

"It's good pay, Mama, and the travel isn't that bad."

Maricel's mother was frowning. It was a frown Maricel knew well, which meant she was living on the edge of doing and not doing this job. If she made one slight wrong move, her mother would forbid her from continuing the work. Her father always deferred to her mother, so there would be no appeal if that happened. She sensed she was safe for now, but there were no guarantees.

She was glad her grandmother hadn't told her mother about the mysterious stranger she asked her to find out about. She was sure her mother would disapprove.

The Priest

Maricel arrived at the Elita at 7:30 a.m. with a bounty of supplies—fresh fruit, eggs, ham, and bread—creating a breakfast large enough to serve as the day's only meal. The past two mornings, she skillfully prepared eggs to order—fried, over easy, or hard-boiled—accompanied by toasted bread with fresh butter, milk, and rich Cuban coffee served as espresso or "con leche." As she cooked, the apartment was filled with melodious Cuban tunes, creating an exotic atmosphere that, combined with the apartment's views and ambiance, made for an unforgettable experience.

Phoebe and Mera soon discovered that a big part of the charm of their stay in Havana was the morning breakfast ritual. Maricel, a beautiful young woman who could communicate in English and Spanish, kept them on their toes as the morning menu was reviewed and choices were made.

While neither Phoebe nor Mera was in the habit of eating such large, hearty breakfasts, there wasn't any way to resist the aromas coming out of the kitchen when Maricel started preparing the ham, eggs, and coffee.

Fresh fruit was also on the menu. Mangoes, bananas, pineapple, and mamay had all been picked that morning or the night before. The smell of the ham and eggs was intoxicating, and the fresh fruit tasted amazing.

Maricel put the plates of food on the table, and Phoebe and Mera started to eat.

"How much food do you and your family trade for, Maricel?" Phoebe asked. "If you don't mind my asking."

"No, I do not mind. My family used to live in the country. We lived out toward Cienfuegos. We couldn't farm enough to make a living, so when my mother's sister got an apartment, we came to live with her in Havana. At least here, we can earn a living and buy things we need. My father works for the road department, and my mother works in the hospital. With the work I do, we manage."

"How big is the apartment, Maricel?" Phoebe asked.

"It is four rooms, and actually, it is in Guanabacoa.

"Four bedrooms?"

"No, four rooms. Two bedrooms, a kitchen, and a living room. Oh, and a bathroom, of course."

"Maricel, forgive me for being so direct, but how many people live in the apartment?" Mera asked.

"All together, there are eleven of us."

Phoebe and Mera looked at each other for a long moment.

"Maricel, this food is delicious," Mera said, forcing a smile.

Since arriving in Cuba, Mera has seen the beauty of the architecture, the people, and the culture. She also saw the decay and the struggles of everyday life. Julian had opened her eyes, or so she thought, to the people's struggles. Maricel gave her a new perspective and way of looking at the people, politics, and culture. Before arriving, Mera thought she had no preconceived notion of the island. She had also convinced herself she would take the island and Havana without judgment. Now, she had to admit being in Havana was nothing like what she had imagined.

After breakfast, Mera and Phoebe went to their rooms.

Mera finished getting ready just as Julian and I arrived.

"Are you ladies ready?" I asked as we walked in.

"We are," Phoebe said, walking out of her room into the living area. "But before we go, there's someone I'd like you to meet. Maricel, come meet our friends."

Maricel walked out of the kitchen and into the living room, where everyone was standing.

"Maricel, this is Max and Julian," Phoebe said. "Julian is Cuban, as you might have guessed, and Max is originally from Key West. I'm not sure we mentioned to you that we are all here for the Hemingway colloquium."

"Buenos dais," Maricel said. "I am so happy to meet you both. *Señor* Julian, where are you from originally?"

"I am from San Francisco de Paula," Julian said. "I left the island when I was very young."

"Julian's father worked for Ernest Hemingway at the Finca Vigía," Phoebe said. "He was Hemingway's majordomo for many years and was with the author until he left Cuba in 1961."

"It is an honor to meet you," Maricel said. "Are you a priest?"

The question came from nowhere and took Phoebe and Mera by surprise. I knew where this was going.

"I am not a priest," Julian said. "My father was a priest. It's funny you ask."

"Perhaps I have been too forward. I apologize. But you look like a priest," Maricel said. "I should say I feel you are a priest if that makes sense."

"It makes sense," Julian said. "There are several practitioners in my family."

"Practicing Palo?" Maricel asked.

"Yes," Julian answered. "Palo Monte. Otherwise known as Las Reglas de Congo."

Julian added the last part more for his friends than for Maricel, who he sensed knew quite a bit about the Palo religion.

"And you are not a 'practitioner,' as you call it?"

"No, not as my father."

"Did Mr. Hemingway know about your father's religion?"

"It is hard to say. Max and I think so," Julian said. "We suspect it would have been hard for him not to have known. Also, certain references in his writing suggest he had some knowledge of the religion and its symbolism and powers."

"You know a lot about the Palo religion," I said. Julian tells me not many women practice it. Do you have a connection? Or does a family member have a connection?"

"All the men in my family have practiced Palo Monte for as long as I can remember. I remember seeing the *prendas* full of the Palos; they were strange to me as a small girl. I didn't understand until later what was happening with the symbolism and the rituals. Then, I became fascinated and wanted to learn, but as you say, it is not a religion that is friendly to women."

"Now I'm curious, Maricel," Phoebe said. "If you don't mind me asking, what do you practice?"

"No, I do not mind. I practice what you would know as Santeria. Santeria is much more welcoming for women, and I hope to be considered a Santera one day. Cubans don't talk about these things because all of these religions have negative connotations in Western cultures."

"Palo has traditionally been a male-dominated religion," Julian said. "Machismo is a big part of the religion's culture and practice, although it has been overhyped for a long time. My father was not so focused on male dominance in the practice. Old beliefs are hard to overcome."

"I hate to break this up," I said. But we need to go. "The taxi is waiting downstairs, and even accounting for Cuban time; the conference will start soon."

"Yes, we need to go," Julian said. "It was nice to meet you, Maricel. I hope to see you again. I know you are taking good care of our friends."

"I hope to see you again, too, Julian," Maricel said. "I'm sure your father was a great man. I'm sure he was proud of you, and I know you miss him."

Julian smiled at Maricel. "You are too kind," he said.

Max and Julian walked into the hallway to the fourth floor to collect their things.

"How did she know?" I asked.

"How did she know what?" Julian asked.

"How did she know your father is dead."

"I don't know," Julian said. "I must have said something."

"I don't think so," I said. "I was listening pretty closely."

"Maybe she assumed," Julian said.

"Seems a little strange," I said. "I got the sense she knew more than she was letting on."

"Don't be so paranoid," Julian said. But he was thinking the same thing. How did she know?

He grabbed his satchel and headed for the front door of the apartment.

"Come on, Max, let's go," Julian said. "We are going to be late for our screening."

Between
Key West and Cuba

This morning's ride was a dark green, 1952 Chevrolet Bel Air. The driver was Manuel, or Manny, as he liked to be called.

"Ok, what the hell was that?" Phoebe asked as the taxi pulled away from the curb. "How in the hell did Maricel know to ask about your religious practices, Julian?"

"I don't know," Julian said. "I'm not sure why she would have any idea about me or my father."

"Seemed out of the blue," Mera said.

"It did," I agreed. "Did she ask any questions yesterday?"

"No, but she didn't see you guys yesterday," Phoebe said. "She is the sweetest person. We have gotten to know her a little over the past few days. She lives with her parents and some extended family in Guanabacoa."

"Eleven of them share an apartment," Phoebe continued. "They all moved in together in Guanabacoa. From what I gather from our conversation last night, this is common in Havana and the surrounding suburbs."

"Yes, exactly," Julian said. "Now you see the problem, up close and personal, as the saying goes."

In front of the Riviera, the 1950s and Hemingway were back front and center.

Julian paid Manny, and we got out of the car.

"I don't think I will ever get tired of walking into this entrance," Phoebe said.

"I know," Mera agreed. "It is like a time machine."

"Time machine, my ass," I said, smiling. "You two are looking for Julio and a mojito as soon as you can get your hands on one."

"Don't be so cynical," Phoebe said. "Also, I hate it when you have us figured out."

The short documentary Julian and I produced was on the program this morning. About the connection between Key West and Cuba, it used Hemingway's writing to put that connection in context.

The moderator introduced Julian, and he made a brief introduction to the film in Spanish. The room darkened, and the documentary started.

When the film ended, there was an enthusiastic round of applause.

"I hope you all have enjoyed the film," the moderator said in Spanish. "I have asked Julian and Max to come to the front and answer any questions you may have."

There were several questions, and Julian answered them to the audience's satisfaction. The screening was a success, and we both left the session feeling satisfied that our efforts had been successful.

"I think that went well," I said as we walked to the back of the room.

"I think so, too," Julian said.

Phoebe and Mera congratulated us on the reception the film garnered.

"What now?" Phoebe asked.

"Jesús is taking us to Regla for the afternoon," Julian said. "I hope no one is disappointed if they were to miss this afternoon's sessions."

"That's fine with me," Mera said. "I want to see the church and hear the stories."

"Me too," Phoebe added.

"Let's go before someone invites us to lunch," I said.

We collected our belongings and went to the front of the hotel where Jesús was waiting. He was waving, smiling, and looking excited to see his new friends.

Julian climbed into the front seat, and Phoebe, me, and Mera crowded into the back.

Regla

Jesús navigated the harbor, tracing a path by Plaza de Armas and Plaza de San Francisco to the right and the waterfront unfolding on the left. Alongside, remnants of the once-confining stone wall, now breached, hinted at the old city's expansion beyond its original boundaries into the surrounding landscape.

As the car traveled along the harbor, moving steadily south and east, the conversation turned to Regla and its place in Cuba and Havana's cultural and religious communities.

"Julian, can you tell us about Regla and the church?" Mera asked.

"I have wanted you to see the church and the waterfront for some time," Julian said. "Regla's church exerts its influence over Havana and the expanse of Cuba, weaving its reach from Baracoa and Santiago in the east to the fertile tobacco fields and *mogotés* of Viñales in the west. Despite its unassuming exterior, it contains a surprisingly grand space, with a soaring ceiling ascending to one hundred feet. Painted a light blue, the ceiling and altar symbolize the Virgin's profound connection to the sea. Regla, a hub of centuries-old slave trade, witnessed the arrival of untold numbers of Africans to Cuba. The church, central to the syncretizing of African, Taíno, and Catholic religions, is a testament to this history. Annually, on September 8, a festival gathers the faithful for a procession, marking a poignant tradition."

"Is it a festival to celebrate her, or are there other purposes? You talk about blending the three religions, which is a lot to pack into a belief system," Phoebe said.

"The festival embodies Yemayá," Julian explained. "Yemayá, Mother Earth, embraces all as her children, including those who are fish. A woman's amniotic fluid mirrors the essence of seawater, forging a spiritual bond with the sea. Simply put, Yemayá is akin to the Virgin Mary. Rivers give life, and her connection to the sea in Cuba and the Caribbean emanates from her link with Olokun, the ruler of the deep waters. The countless lives lost in Olokun's domain led people to seek solace in Yemayá, like turning to a mother for comfort. Within Caribbean Orisha faiths, Yemayá melds with Our Lady of Regla. In Yorubaland, she reigns over the Ogun River, with the Niger River holding significance as well."

"Oh my," Phoebe said as she looked at Mera. "Caridad and the rings."

"What?" I asked.

"Nothing," Mera said. "She was just someone we met on the plane—a fascinating lady."

Julian was busy trying to gather his thoughts and missed the exchange between me, Phoebe, and Mera. Phoebe gave Mera another glance. Both their minds were racing now.

Jesús pulled in front of the church, and Julian asked him to stop at the entrance, where the street intersected the church property on the right and the docks and waterfront on the left, where the boats came in to offload their human cargo.

"Julian, tell them what happens in September," I said.

"During the September celebrations, it is always interesting to see the number of priests and priestesses of Ocha and Palo, priests of Ifá and Abakúa, and spiritualists, all who have been wrongly classified as witches over the centuries, marching under the banner of 'Mama Azul,' the Blue Mother. It's not only the descendants of Africans who carry the image of Our Lady through the town, stopping at the houses of the great Santeros so she can receive an offering, but also at the Abakuá lodges, fanatics of the Virgin visit the town hall and then proceed to the cemetery to greet the dead. Then, in what is the most powerful manifestation of the syncretization—without ever ceasing to consider themselves Catholics—they bathe the *otán,* the sacred stone, the residence of *Yemayá*, in the blood of a ram or chicken in the numerous Orisha house temples on the island."

As he finished his explanation, Julian noticed a man dressed in all white, with a white hat and prominent gold jewelry. He was standing next to the wall surrounding the church.

"Max, can you show Phoebe and Mera the waterfront?" Julian asked. "I want to talk to this gentleman over here by the wall."

"Let's check out the harbor," I said to Mera and Phoebe.

We exited the car and crossed the street to the docks.

Julian walked over to the man dressed in white, who looked unassuming as he stood by the wall.

"Excuse me," Julian said to him. "May I ask your name?"

"My name is Abél," the man said.

"And you are Abakúa?" Julian asked.

The man looked apprehensive and nodded slightly in the affirmative.

"I'm sorry; I didn't mean to startle you," Julian said. "I'm looking for someone, and I hope you can help me.

"I'm not sure how that can be," Abél said. "But I will try."

"My name is Julian. It is nice to meet you. I am looking for a priest or priestess. Whoever this person is can help me with something I am trying to do here on the island. They are powerful; at least, I hope so. I hope they are well-known so you might know them.

"What is it you are trying to do?" Abél asked. "Knowing might make it easier for me to know who you are looking for."

"There is a particular ceremony I would like to have performed," Julian said. "An ancient ceremony of Taíno origin. Not a blessing but a ritual, something that can help me explore the other side."

Julian knew he was taking a chance to be so explicit with someone he just met, but now was not a time to be timid. He needed to make contact and didn't have time to waste.

"There is only one person in Regla who can help with such a thing," Abél said. "I saw her praying in the church earlier, near the front. I can take you inside and see if she is still there."

"That would be wonderful," Julian said.

They walked to the church and entered through the side door. Julian stopped to admire the altar and the statue of the Virgin. He was always awestruck by the sight of her.

Abél took several steps into the sanctuary and waited a few moments for his eyes to adjust to the relative darkness inside. Julian stood patiently and waited for him to look around.

As they were waiting, a diminutive woman dressed in all white, complete with a white turban, stood up in a pew three rows back from the front of the church.

Caridad sensed Julian's presence when he walked into the sanctuary. She turned and looked for him. Maricel had given her a description, and she gasped when she saw the tall, dark man dressed in white.

Frozen by the realization that Julian was the son she had been dreaming about, it took her a few moments to recover. She met Julian's gaze and gave a brief nod, making her way to the end of the pew, kneeling to genuflect.

"There she is," Abél said. "Her name is Caridad."

Julian didn't need the confirmation; he knew she was the person he was looking for when their eyes met.

Caridad stayed on one knee at the end of the pew for longer than would have been customary. She had taken the time to gather herself. Once she felt in control of her emotions, she started walking toward Julian. She was smiling as the soft, trilling sound she made when she walked reverberated through the church.

Julian heard the sound and felt a vibration he knew was coming from the other side.

When she was close, Caridad reached out her hand.

"The man of my dreams," Caridad said, smiling.

Julian understood the humor. He smiled back.

"My name is Caridad," she said. "I think you have been looking for me. I know I have been looking for you."

"Yes," Julian said. "And you are the angel of my dreams."

He extended his hand.

Caridad took Julian's left hand, turning it palm up. In her right hand, she was holding a small vert-de-gris ring. The patina and artistry betrayed its ancient origins.

"This is for you," she said. "It is the last one my family owns and now belongs to you. It completes one journey and begins another."

Julian accepted it without question. To refuse the gift would be an insult to her and to the gesture she was making. He turned it over in his hand, inspecting it in a way that demonstrated respect and appreciation.

"It looks ancient," Julian said.

"Yes, it is," Caridad said. "Your two friends each have one."

"How is it you know my friends?" Julian asked.

"I met them on the plane three days ago. I gave each of them a ring like the one you are holding. I have dreamt of your coming to Havana, and now you are here. Until today, I wasn't sure you were the one I was looking for, but your desire to find me proves we were meant to meet."

"What is the purpose of it?" Julian asked as he continued to examine the ring.

"It is a connection to the other side. A marker for the one who possesses it, providing a means of communication. It represents a merging of the Taíno and African religions. The ring is from the Niger River region and complements the shells and sacred markings that our Taíno ancestors used for the same reason over the centuries."

"It is an amazing relic. I am honored that you think I'm worthy of possessing it. Do you know why I am looking for you?" Julian asked.

"No. Only that you are looking for me."

Caridad knew from her dream that Julian was searching for his father in the afterlife. She also knew she could assist in several ways, from the simplest to the most powerful. Rather than put words in his mouth, she wanted him to explain what he wanted.

"There is an old ritual, a ceremony that allows communication with those who have passed to the other side," Julian said. "I learned of this from my father, a Palo priest."

"The *Areyto*," Caridad said. "I am familiar with it. It requires particular expertise and involves ritual drumming and someone familiar with the ritual dance used to summon the *Orishas* and those ancestors you hope to contact."

"I understand the music and the dance are complex and critical to the success of opening the path," Julian said.

"Well, the drumming is a particular cadence, which is not so hard to perform," Caridad said. "But the dance, handed down for centuries, is difficult and must be performed precisely."

"What is the origin?" Julian asked. "I assume it is primarily Taíno."

"It is Taíno," Caridad said. "As with all religions practiced on the island, there are also significant African influences.

Catholicism has cloaked all this knowledge and expertise since the Spanish invasion."

"Do you perform the dance?" Julian asked.

"Oh my, no," Caridad said smiling. "A much younger woman dances the *Areyto*. It has been handed down from generation to generation, and my family has passed the choreography down to each succeeding generation. It has been a long time since anyone has danced as part of the ceremony you are requesting. Instead, it has been passed down and performed in other, less profound rituals and celebrations."

"Is there someone who can perform the dance now?"

"Yes. My granddaughter can perform it. I have been teaching her the steps since she was a little girl. She has been performing parts of it at celebrations and gatherings for many years. You have met her."

Julian thought for a moment. It was all making sense now.

"Maricel?" Julian asked.

"Yes. How did you know?"

Julian smiled, remembering his conversation with Maricel at the apartment.

"That certainly answers many questions about my conversation with her," Julian said.

Caridad looked at Julian with sympathy. She knew he understood what he was asking her to do was extraordinary and dangerous.

"You know, the stories about the performance of the ritual and its aftermath, told and retold over the centuries, have been stories of mixed outcomes. Some were positive, but some led to unintended or disastrous results and consequences," Caridad said. "Our families are descended from the Taíno tribes that were here when Columbus arrived."

"Yes, I am aware of this," Julian said. "My father was careful to explain our family origins in great detail. He was careful to make sure I understood the bloodlines."

"We are both embarking on a journey with no guaranteed outcome," Caridad said. "It is as likely to produce a bad outcome as a good one."

"I understand," Julian said. "But you can't predetermine a good and bad outcome, can you? Our destinies flow from the choices and decisions we make. If you agree to help me in this matter, I can assure you the outcome, whatever it may be, will be the outcome we are all supposed to achieve."

Caridad looked at Julian. She knew he was right, but the idea that she might regret helping him, regardless of how he may feel about the outcome, was weighing on her.

"I will help you with this," she said. "Because our destinies are intertwined and have been for some time—maybe forever. I have Maricel to think of. Providing the path to the other side will fall to her, and this is no small undertaking."

"I understand," Julian said again. "Let's agree right now that we will not do anything that jeopardizes her safety and well-being. It's the last thing I would want to do."

"We are agreed then," Caridad said. "I will help you. We will help you. There is one more thing."

"Please tell me," Julian said.

"None of us know the outcome of this journey," Caridad said. "We cannot know what the *Orishas* have in mind, nor do we know the best outcome for us. As you say, there can be different perspectives on the same destinies, and how we ultimately come out of this will be something we cannot control."

"Agreed," Julian said. "Now, all we need is a place."

"That will be up to you, Maestro," Caridad said.

"Then I will let you know when I know," Julian said. "I have an idea and will soon know if it is feasible. I assume Jesús is connected to you somehow and can deliver a message?"

"Yes," Caridad said, smiling. "You do not miss anything, do you."

"I try not to," Julian said. "Now, if you excuse me, I will give my friends a tour of this beautiful church."

Julian started to walk away from Caridad, but he thought of one last question.

"I understand why you gave me a ring. I assume it has something to do with the ceremony and the connection to the other side. But why did you give Phoebe and Mera a ring before you met me or knew who I was?" Julian asked.

"I had a strong sense they were connected to you, so I wanted them to be connected to me," Caridad said. "Whoever receives the rings connects to me in a way I cannot explain. The two I gave to Mera and Phoebe were two of the last three in my possession. Theirs, and the one I gave you, spent many months in my Nganga. Now, we will be connected no matter where you are, assuming you can open yourselves up to the possibility."

"My friend Max doesn't have one," Julian said.

Caridad smiled at Julian, taking a long moment to respond.

"Max doesn't need one," Caridad said as she turned to walk away. "Maximilian must find his way. It is his destiny."

The Ties that Bind

And here, the carnival Havana lights
Are hung along the shore and thread the sea
At night, while in the old distillery,
Destroyed by fire, the moonlight on the stones
Transforms the floor to marble, and the rows
Of crossbeams make a multiple crucifixion
Where hanged men tread their first macabre dance
And love commits idolatry in the dark.

— *Phillip Murray*

"Max, your mother was born in Guanabacoa?" Phoebe asked.

"Yes, her father was a doctor. He died when she was young, and her mother remarried. They moved to Key West when she was five years old. My grandmother was baptized here in the church. I have a copy of the baptismal certificate."

We were standing in the church, looking at the ornate altar. In all her glory, the Virgin of Regla statue was the prominent feature. The black Madonna was the center of attention in the church and throughout the country.

"The virgin is the pinnacle of the syncretized religions," Julian said. "Remember, our Lady of Regla represents the Virgin Mary, Yemayá, and Mother Earth."

"Where does your father fit into this religious pantheon, Julian?" Mera asked.

"Most importantly, as a Palo Priest," Julian said. "He had Taíno, African and Spanish blood. His heritage goes back to the Taíno villages that were here when Columbus arrived."

"His family had been practicing the Indigenous religion for centuries," I said. "It started with the Taíno origin stories and then adapted with the arrival of the Africans with their religions. They were under constant scrutiny from the Spanish, the Portuguese, and the English. Christianity, preferably in the form of Catholicism, was the only acceptable religion."

"So, they adapted and took their beliefs underground?" Phoebe asked.

"Not exactly," Julian said. "They adapted to the Catholic structure. They were hiding their religion in plain sight. Their altars were made up of everyday objects. China from England, rocks, small totems that looked like everyday things. These items were consecrated and arranged on a table in their personal spaces. It has become much more open now, without the persecution or the negative reputation."

"There are still some very negative connotations around what is commonly called Santeria," I said. "The image of animal sacrifice and the use of human skulls in some of the ceremonies puts people off."

"Yes, even though these things were practiced and documented in the Christian bible, it never mattered," Julian added. "The Taíno were considered primitive, even though the Europeans knew they had their language, culture, and religion. None of that mattered in the end because Spain, England, Portugal, and all of the other so-called civilized countries looked down on the Indigenous people they encountered everywhere on the islands."

"The last fateful step was to import African slaves to take the place of the Taíno, who died by disease or at the hands of their overlords after they had been enslaved," I said. "This is the site of the unspeakable horrors and the divine intervention. Their faith carried them through despite the relentless oppression. But it was not the faith of their oppressors; it was the faith of their ancestors. It is a testament to the human spirit and how religion and faith can help people endure and flourish."

"It is a beautiful church," Mera said. "I think the Madonna is beautiful."

"It is sacred ground," Julian said.

"We should probably go," I said. "We have to be at Alex's house by seven."

"Thank you for sharing," Phoebe said. "It is a special place for both of you."

Jesús was waiting at the curb when we arrived. We rode in silence back along the waterfront, past the Plaza and the old wall no longer guarding the city. We were each lost in our thoughts, so the silence wasn't noticed. It was as if the drums and claves had silenced themselves in deference to the history and the tragedy hanging heavy in the air. Havana rarely went silent but riding in the old, green Chevrolet at that moment was a welcome break and a chance to contemplate the Cuban people's spirit and tenacity.

Sacred Space

Moving gracefully across the sand flats, the bull shark navigates through the patches of sea grass growing close to shore. Approaching the ancient coral formations, she anticipates the calm of the shallow sea floor, where she will soon settle, patiently awaiting the sunset.

A hundred yards to the south, in the big two-story house, sitting inside the mangroves and four feet above the high-water mark, the doctor speaks extremely low and somberly.

"Angelita, we will be leaving in a few days," he says.

It's 1961, and Angelita Blanco doesn't understand why there is such a rush to leave. The doctor has been practicing medicine in the pueblo for twenty years. Employed by the Perla family since the age of fifteen, she does more than just cleaning and cooking; she considers herself an integral part of their extended family. The bond she shares with the doctor's three children feels as strong as if they were her own.

The house was built in 1919 by Alejandro Perla, a young Cuban aviator born in Key West to Cuban exiles. Alejandro was one of the first to fly from Key West to Cuba. His father was a big supporter of Jose Martí and Cuban independence. At the time of Alejandro's historic first flight, he had on board a statue of the Virgin of Cobra, a miniature painting of Oshun, the Orisha of water, and the Cuban flag. Jose Marti had carried them with him during his travels in Florida, raising money for the Cuban cause.

Alejandro did not make landfall in Havana on that first flight. Instead, he landed in heavy winds and rough seas just outside the port of Mariel, where sailors rescued him. He took his survival of the harrowing end to his historic trip as a sign that he had arrived home.

Shortly after that, he purchased property on the waterfront near his landing. There were rumors that the property had been the site of ancient Taíno rituals, but Alejandro considered these stories quaint folklore. Shortly after acquiring the property, he built a house with a view toward Key West. It sat back from the shore to avoid disturbing the rock formations arranged in concentric circles. The larger circle had a diameter of approximately 100 feet, and the smaller circle was used as a fire pit. At least, that was the story Alejandro heard when he bought the property. It was said Alejandro would sit for hours on the second-floor porch and imagine he could see Key West.

When Alejandro bought the property, in addition to the rock formations, there was a small wooden house near the shore and west of where he would eventually build his house. This modest wooden structure was the home of the Blanco family, who had lived on the small plot of land for the last 200 years. The Blancos were of primarily African descent and looked like the indigenous Taíno tribes that inhabited the island before the Europeans arrived. It was said there were no longer any Taíno people on the island, having been wiped out by the war and sickness brought by the Europeans. The Cubans knew better.

Constantine Prueda was a physician and the husband of Consuelo Prueda Perla, Alejandro's daughter, and his only offspring. Ownership of the house had transferred to Consuelo after her father's passing in 1950, and the couple had lived and thrived in the house for the last eight years.

Their life and marriage were vibrant, intensifying once they moved into the house.

Their parties were legendary, and the guests would be entertained by the best musicians and fed by the best chefs in Havana. The conversation would go well into the morning of the following day, and Constantine and Consuelo were legendary in Mariel and Havana as extraordinary hosts.

Now, decisions and plans have been made for the first time in a long time without including Angelita. Her inclusion in the past served as a testament to her closeness to them; now, this unspoken rule has been violated. She helps the family pack what few things they can take with them, hopefully making the journey less traumatic and the exile less permanent.

"When will you be back?" she asks.

"I don't know," the doctor says. There was a sadness in his voice that Angelita rarely heard. "I don't think it will be any time soon."

The doctor hands Angelita a paper, signed and notarized, giving her permission to live in the house.

"I don't know if this will do you any good, Angelita, but it is the best I can do."

Alex Ortega is Angelita Blanco's grandson. He is a successful artist and printmaker, and he is hard at work in his studio, which occupies the upstairs bedroom of the same two-story house. The doctor and his family fled fifty-eight years ago. Twenty-five years ago, Angelita told Alex the story.

Alex thinks about his grandmother when he's working, and she shows up often in his work. Some manifestations are unusual and symbolic, and some are predictable. She is always guiding him. Alex has many memories of his grandmother, from living with her and also from the stories she told about her life before he was born. She was a constant presence when she was alive, and she is a constant presence still.

Alex is deep in thought as the gouge slips slowly and deliberately through the pencil line drawn on the scavenged piece of plywood that will be used to print the image he is creating. His hand moves steadily as the thin sliver of wood curls up and out of the surface. The image he is making is meant to represent his grandmother's pelvis in skeletal form. As the outer curve of the hip bone takes shape, He thinks of one of her many instructions for him.

"You will never have anything as valuable as your friends or those you love."

She had been gone fifteen years, and Alex can still hear her voice as if she is standing beside him.

The awls and gouges Alex uses to make the grooves and shallow flat places are sharp, and the plywood is thin. The technique always makes for slow progress, but Alex loves this part of the process. His images are always dense and intricate, full of sea and land animals and birds, plants, and human-made objects. Finely drawn, there is always an element of surprise, and combining human objects and nature creates unusual and surprising connections.

The familiar shadow catches his eye as he straightens up and walks to the back of the house. He can see it from the doorway of the second-story porch, moving in the clear shallows, even though it must be almost one hundred yards offshore. Its movement is deliberate, and he estimates the shark to be about six feet long. This isn't the first time he has seen it patrolling off the beach, so he thinks this must be the same shark, and this is its territory.

He feels the sea breeze as he walks onto the porch, a refreshing shift from the intense concentration inside. Memories flood the wide expanse, not of his youth but of stories told by his grandmother. Stories of family love and care always echo in the porch's vastness. Alex finds comfort in these narratives, deepening his love for his grandmother and providing a salve for the pain of her loss. The porch becomes a haven intertwined with cherished recollections and newfound inspiration.

The shark moves slowly to the west, and Alex can hear his grandmother's voice as she tells the story:

"Angelita, take the house. You will need a bigger place to live, and it will be of no use to me once we are gone." The doctor explained to Angelita that the house would not belong to anyone once he and his family were gone. "I don't know what the government will do, but I don't think they will be too concerned with what goes on this far from Havana, at least not soon."

Angelita couldn't believe there would be no quick return for her second family. She knew she was being naïve, but the idea this was the last time she would see them was unthinkable.

"This can't be true," she said.

But as she said it, she knew her voice was betraying her doubts. The doctor looked at her with sadness and understanding.

"You will be ok," he said. "You have to look out for your family now."

Angelita could feel the emotion well inside her, even though she had promised herself she wouldn't cry. It was true; she had her own family to look after. Her children would need her now in these uncertain times. Many things were happening, and no one knew what they meant, least of all Angelita. She had no interest in politics and less in what was happening in Havana.

And so, the house sat empty, its wide porches empty of visitors and rooms empty of family. When he was growing up, Alex never understood why his grandmother hadn't moved into the doctor's house. Instead, she stayed in the tiny house that was more of a shack than a house. Over the years, as he understood she was the guiding force in his life, he also understood that force had been about a keen sense of duty and a strong sense of home and family.

"What good would it do me to move into such a large house," his grandmother had asked when Alex questioned her. "What would the doctor say and do if he came home?"

Alex knew it was pointless arguing with her; she had told him many times that she could not accept that the doctor and his family were not coming home.

He was always sad when he thought about his grandmother waiting in her tiny house for the doctor's return. Of course, it never happened for her, like the reunions have never happened for so many Cubans who remained on the island. Their eternity had been lived out and was still being lived out, one year at a time. *It is funny and sad*, he thought, *the Cuban people had been waiting an eternity, one day, one month, and one year at a time, for the last sixty years.*

Alex felt the breeze on his face. The shark was farther out to sea now, and he could barely see it as it moved slowly out of sight. He imagined seeing the coastline of the United States ninety miles to the north, thinking again of his grandmother. If it hadn't been for her, his work may not have resonated with those who now wanted to own it.

Alex wondered what that day was like—the day the doctor and his family packed up and moved out of their beautiful house on the water. That day, they took what little of their belongings they could and left their beloved Cuba. So much of their lives had been left behind. Most of their personal belongings, the artwork and furniture, the silverware and china, and the clothing they couldn't carry in the small suitcases allotted to them, were still in the house.

All of these things, and the memories that went with them, had been left in the care of his grandmother. Alex vaguely remembers her wandering through the house like a silent, watchful angel. The artwork on the walls is a testament to the Cuban spirit and the place where he first let the images and the need to create enter his soul. He can see his grandmother walking the hallways and entering the parlor full of dark, Cuban mahogany furniture, taffeta, and silk fabrics. What must her memories have been of the doctor and his family, entertaining guests with conversations about art and literature and the travels made and still to come, or sitting silently listening to the great Cuban musicians as they filled the humid, tropical air with the sounds of piano and percussion and strings played out on the victrola sounding thin and reedy and nothing like they sounded in the great music halls in Havana.

As Angelita moved through the rooms, did she notice the grand chandeliers hanging like crystal sentinels, casting a pale-yellow light? Did she think about fine English china and the sterling silver serving and dining pieces, requiring constant care in the humid subtropical climate, the care she would have provided? Alex wondered what she would be thinking, moving into the kitchen with its great ovens, each used for a different purpose. The smell of warm bread and pork, yucca thick with garlic and olive oil would have filled the house. How long did the smells and sounds take to leave the house and Angelita's memory?

Even though she had often explained her sense of confusion and dread, Angelita never told Alex how long the memories lasted, not as slim, vague threads but as visceral physical sounds and smells. She had no way of knowing if the doctor and his family made it safely to the US or if they had been harassed on their way out of Cuba. There were so many rumors about the new government confiscating all property. She was convinced someone would come and inventory all of the doctor's belongings, down to the last fork, spoon, family photograph, and memento.

It never happened. No one ever came to take the house in Mariel. Alex could not understand what happened next, but he knew Angelita had spent her last day in the house before she decided it was time to leave.

Echoes

Back in the studio, Alex continued to work on his grandmother's image, focusing on her pelvis. As the gouge traced the line of her hip, he wondered about her final day. Did she wake up with a sense of purpose, mapping her path through the house, reminiscing about paintings and furniture placements? Did thoughts of the doctor's family flood her mind? Leaning over the plywood, the gouge continues to reveal her spinal cord, following the drawn lines. Imagining Angelita walking to the shore, past mangroves, and into shallow waters, he wonders if there were moments of reflection. Did she pause, thinking about where she was going? Did the sand underfoot and the coolness of the water occupy her thoughts? Carving the fifth lumbar vertebra, Alex moved deliberately, still contemplating the mysteries that swirled around his grandmother's final day— did she, at some point, gaze northward, pondering the doctor's fate?

The fourth vertebra began to appear as the next, thin, sliver of wood worked its way up and out of the panel with the gentle coaxing of the gouge. Alex thought about what might have happened next. He thought Angelita would have taken a moment to look out to sea, understanding the seriousness of her next move. The third vertebra began to appear, and Alex imagined the coolness of the water and how his grandmother felt when it came up around her as she slowly walked out into the shallows. Was she looking for the sandy spot, he wondered?

Did she have a place where she was headed outside the shallow water, or was she thinking of something or someone else? The second vertebra was nearing completion, and Alex thought about his grandmother swimming now, with the cool, calm water surrounding her. She would have been far out, past the shallows and into the coral rock formations. Did she turn around and look back? Did she think about her children and her grandchildren? What kept her going? Farther out, the water is too deep to stand, and there must have been a moment when she had a second thought. Did she think what she was doing was best for her? Was it best for her family?

Alex knows she swam for quite some time because a neighbor spotted her in the deep water. Out past the coral and into the deeper blue water, the current would pick her up and carry her north and east. Depending on the day, the currents could have been closer in. Did Angelita wait for the current to be close? Was that what made that day the day?

Alex was done carving. The first vertebra of the lumbar region had been outlined, stacked neatly on the others, and ending in space. This is how Angelita would live in Alex's latest dream world. More details would be added, but that would be for another day. He stood for a moment admiring his work. He felt the sea breeze as he walked out onto the porch.

Alex was looking at the beach and thinking about his grandmother. He looked past the shore and toward the horizon, out past the shallow flats and the sand bar. He could no longer see the bull shark moving slowly along the sandy bottom between the ancient coral. *The shark has given up and moved on,* he thought. But he knew this couldn't be true. Sharks never give up; they always come back.

Black Witch Moth

In the night's sky over the river of the dead, they fly,
cutting the threads that tie people to life . . .

— *Deborah Lee*

"I have to do laundry," Phoebe said back on the 11th floor of the Elita. "I have run out of options for the rest of the trip."

Everyone was excited to be going to dinner with Alex and Delia. It promised a pleasant change in mood and energy compared to the visit to Regla.

Phoebe gathered her clothes and headed to the enclosed porch with the washer and dryer. She found the soap and opened the small door to the front load machine.

Mera had gone to her room when she heard the commotion. Phoebe let out a blood-curdling scream.

"Oh, my God! It's a bat! Get away from me! Get away from me!"

Mera jumped up and ran to the sound of Phoebe's screaming. When she arrived, Phoebe's arms were flailing, and she was waving a pair of her underwear at a big, black, flying object.

"What the hell is it?" Mera yelled.

"It's a bat!" Phoebe yelled back. "Get this thing off of me!"

"It's not on you," Mera yelled. "Also, I don't think it's a bat!"

"What the hell are you talking about," Phoebe said, still yelling. "Look at the size of it!"

"I see the size of it," Mera said. "But I don't think it's a bat. It looks more like a moth!" she screamed.

"I don't care what it is; I want it out of here!" Phoebe said.

Mera looked around for something to shoo the bat, moth, or whatever from the porch.

"Stop flailing with the damn underwear!" Mera yelled. "Open one of those windows so I can get this thing out of here."

Along the outside wall of the porch was a row of windows that looked original to the building. They were two feet wide by four feet tall. There were five of them, and each had its own crank handle.

"Shit!" Phoebe said. "Shit, Shit, Shit!"

Phoebe backed to the window, not taking her eye off the bat, and fumbled with the crank. It was an old crank-out window, and upon cursory inspection, it didn't look like it intended to open.

"It's coming after me!" Phoebe said.

"No, it isn't! Stop yelling and crank the window!" Mera yelled.

Phoebe clutched at the lever and tried to turn it.

"Shit!" Phoebe said. "It's not cranking."

"Turn it the other way," Mera said as calmly as she could.

Phoebe turned in the other direction. At first, there was no movement, and then, suddenly, the crank handle broke free and started to turn.

"It's opening!" Phoebe shouted. "Come on, bat! Get the hell out of here!"

While Phoebe was struggling with the window, Mera looked around for something to coax the moth out of the apartment. She found a grease screen in the kitchen and was now armed with a large paddle that she could use to shepherd the moth off the porch.

"Look out," Mera said. "I'm going to try to get him out with this."

Mera was waving the grease screen so that Phoebe could see it.

"Why don't you swat him with it?" Phoebe yelled.

"Because I don't want to piss him off if I miss!" Mera said. "Do you want him mad?"

"No!" Phoebe said. "I want him out of here!"

The moth, giant but not a bat, flew above them, circling as if it didn't know where to go. Disturbed from its sleep, it was now looking for a way to escape the enclosed space. Mera used the screen to guide it toward the open window, and within a few seconds, which seemed like an hour, the moth dove for the open window and was gone.

Phoebe looked at Mera. "Where the hell are Max and Julian when you need them?"

The Messenger

"What the hell is a black witch moth?" Phoebe asked as Jesús headed toward Alex and Delia's house.

"It's what I think you saw, given the description," Julian said.

"It looked like a bat," Phoebe said.

"I'm sure it did," Julian said. "They are large and black, so confusing a mature black witch moth for a bat would be easy. If you were startled and excited, it would be even easier."

"What the hell was it doing in the washing machine?" Phoebe asked.

"They are nocturnal, so they like dark places during the day," Julian said. "In many cultures, the black witch moth is considered a sign, so depending on the country or place, it can represent death or the afterlife. In Native American cultures, it is a messenger from the spirit world. In the Caribbean, it can be good luck or bad luck. It can also be the carriers of death or the profits announcing a new life."

"So basically, you can interpret anything you want from seeing a black witch moth," Mera said.

"Yes, pretty much," Julian said, smiling. "But for me, the black witch moth symbolizes the soul, seeking truth about itself. The person who sees one is looking for themselves. They are on a journey to discover who they are."

"Well, I would have been on a journey out the window if Mera hadn't coaxed it out of the room," Phoebe said.

"Does this have some meaning for you, Julian?" Mera asked. "Or are you pulling our leg?"

"It's all about the circumstance," Julian said. "If someone is already on a spiritual journey, then encountering a moth can be significant. As with everything, it's part of a larger cultural landscape. It is no different from any other superstition or belief."

"One man's superstition is another man's religion," I said.

I was starting to get nervous about the conversation. I still couldn't tell if Julian was serious or entertaining Mera and Phoebe with local folklore and beliefs.

"It's a messenger," I said. "The message is what your religion or beliefs tell you."

"That's true, Max," Julian said. "These moths travel all over the Caribbean. They have been subject to all kinds of interpretations and cultural appropriation. The Cubans never met a story they didn't like, especially if it had some element of the supernatural. As for me, in the context of my journey, I will take this sighting for what it means to me and my belief system."

"And what would that interpretation be?" Phoebe asked.

"The search for my spiritual destiny, I see it as a sign, one sign, that I am on the right path," Julian said. "My interpretation is rooted in the belief my father is trying to reach out to me from the other side. I pursue my destiny by continuing on my journey."

Before Phoebe and Mera could react, Jesús pulled up in front of Alex and Delia's house.

"We're here!" I said with enthusiasm, trying to distract and deflect the conversation.

"I can't wait to see Alex and Delia," Phoebe said. "Mera, this is going to be a treat!"

Alex and Delia

Alex and Delia live on the west side of Havana in an Art Deco-style house on a sloping street. The house also functions as their studio and gallery. For Alex, it's a space used for finishing and printing when he doesn't have the time or the inclination to go to the Mariel house.

When we arrived, Alex was waiting. He came bounding down the stairs, calling out to Julian, Phoebe, and me. He had not met Mera, so he was excited to be introduced.

We moved up the stairs and into the house, where Delia greeted us with big hugs and kisses. Mera was impressed with the décor. A mix of Art Deco and mid-century modern, it was decorated in a way only two artists could accomplish.

I walked to the back of the house with Julian and Alex while Mera and Phoebe took their time, looking in each room and admiring the work so carefully hung on the walls and placed around the spaces.

Alex opened a bottle of Matusalem rum he had saved for a special occasion as Mera, Phoebe, and Delia made their way to the back of the house.

He sprinkled a small amount on the floor behind the bar.

"What's that about?" I asked.

"The first sip always goes to those on the other side," Alex said. "Otherwise, it is bad luck and bad energy."

"Like Julian's totem," I said.

"Yes, exactly, Max," Julian said.

Julian and Mera settled on the couch, and I sat at the small bar with Phoebe. Alex ran into the kitchen and out the back door to check on the food. Once he had everything under control, he returned to the bar.

"Alex, where do you do your work?" Mera asked. I know Delia works from home during the design phase of her process and then in her studio for the actual casting of the pieces. It looks like you have a small studio here, but some of your prints are so large."

"You are observant," Alex said. "I have a larger studio in Mariel. It's a house, part of which I have converted into a studio where I do most of my carving. Julian is familiar with the house."

"Have you been to it?" Mera asked Julian.

"No, I haven't seen it," Julian said. "I have seen pictures, and it is a beautiful house and location. It's right on the water with a view of the ocean and the Gulf Stream. Alex always says what an inspiration it is to his work."

"The house has a long history for me," Alex said. "It is connected to the memory of my grandmother. She worked for a doctor who lived there and left shortly after the revolution. My grandmother was devastated, and she kept the house up for years, waiting for the doctor to return with his family."

"Did he?" Phoebe asked.

"No," Alex said. "He was never coming back. It was a fact my grandmother refused to accept."

"What happened to her?" Phoebe asked. "She must have eventually realized he wasn't coming back."

"She disappeared one day," Alex said. "She was never found."

"Oh my," Mera said. "That must have been awful for you."

"It took me a long time to get over it," Alex said. "Delia will tell you I never did get over it."

"It's your work that betrays the fact you never got over her," Delia said.

"It must be awful to lose someone in mysterious circumstances," Phoebe said.

"They weren't all that mysterious," Delia said. "We are pretty sure she drowned."

"I'm so sorry," Phoebe said. "I can't imagine."

"The night she disappeared, she was wading in the shallows and swimming out into the deeper water," Alex said. "We have no idea what she was doing in the ocean. She didn't leave a note; nothing in the house gave any clues. So, we don't know if it was intentional or if she was confused or disoriented."

Looking at Alex's face, Mera could tell there was a story too painful to tell. She decided to come to his rescue and change the subject.

"What about you, Julian?" Mera asked. "Where and with whom do you commune?" She was smiling as she asked the question.

"Great question," Julian said. "The truth is I have many muses. But I am envious of Alex. He lives here in Havana and has access to the house where his grandmother has such a presence. I left the island as a small boy; the connections are more tenuous. I have relied on my father and mother and my memories as a young boy to make the connection."

"You should come back to Cuba," Alex said. "You can live with us."

Delia raised her eyebrows on her way to the kitchen. Even though she knew it wasn't going to happen. She also knew Alex was serious.

"Better yet, you can stay in the house in Mariel," Alex said. "Maybe you can have some conversations with my grandmother!"

Julian smiled. "I think I would like her very much," he said.

Delia returned and announced dinner was ready.

"Alex, can you help me?" she asked.

We moved to the dining room, which had been set with dishes and silverware from the 1930s.

The room fell silent as we loaded our plates with garlic, oregano, and basil-infused pork, fish marinated in lime juice, fried maduros, black beans, white rice, and a salad dressed in the simplicity of olive oil and vinegar. The meal was a perfect mix of Cuban culinary delights.

Alex opened two bottles of Verdejo from Spain, and the wine, which was light-bodied and tart, was the perfect accompaniment for the fish and the pork.

"Alex, this wine is amazing," Phoebe said. "I don't think I have ever had it."

"Yes!" Alex said excitedly. "It is from Rueda, a place in central Spain. I love the acidity, and it is quite dry. It tastes citrusy, like lime. It makes a great statement with both the pork and the fish."

It was quiet during dinner, but as the meal started to wind down, the conversation picked up where it had left off.

"Alex, tell us about the house in Mariel," Mera said. "It sounds fascinating, and the history of your grandmother living there is so unusual."

"My first thoughts are always of the chandeliers," Alex said. "They are so exquisite, and the light they create in each room takes me to another place outside the physical space.

"Julian, aren't you doing a series that includes chandeliers?" Mera asked.

"I have already done three paintings in the series. The largest is a waterfront scene with tropical rainforest foliage and three chandeliers hovering above the forest. The scene depicts a Taíno village, even though the work has no human figures or structures. I like to think of it as representing the *Zemi spirits* and their presence over the island."

"I wonder if your chandeliers look like the ones in the Mariel house?" Mera asked. "It's fascinating how you both find creative energy from the same iconic thing."

"I remember how my grandmother loved the light and its reflection off the faceted crystals," Alex said. "For me, they also symbolize the arrival of Western civilization in the Caribbean."

"The part about the arrival of Western civilization in Cuba and the Caribbean is where I am going with the work I am currently doing," Julian said. "I think about the arrival of the first Europeans and how they thought they were bringing civilization to people they did not know or respect. The Spaniards, the English, the French, and the Portuguese considered the places they discovered to be appropriated. They felt the same way about the people, even after they realized the Indigenous tribes had quite elaborate societies and religious and political beliefs."

"That's the problematic part, isn't it," Phoebe said. "The mindset of conquering as opposed to discovering."

"Yes, that's it precisely," Julian said. "So, on its most basic level, my work represents the discoverers, bringing the light and civilization to the so-called savages. That's from the perspective of the Europeans. The fact there are no people in the paintings represents the view of the conquerors—the land was a clean slate. It was uninhabited, even though people lived on every island they 'discovered'."

"So, is that the message and theme of the work?" Phoebe asked.

"Yes, that's one side of the story," Julian said. "The other side of the story I'm trying to tell is of the islands' inhabitants. In this case, it's the Taíno living in Baracoa. So, while the chandeliers mean one thing to the Europeans, they mean something entirely different to the Taíno."

"But what is the metaphor for the Taíno?" Phoebe asked. "They would have had no knowledge of chandeliers or what they were used for."

"It's the ships," Julian said. "Imagine seeing the three Spanish ships on the horizon. What would you make of them? How would you interpret them? The Taíno must have seen them as some magic or omen as they neared the shore."

"They must have seemed like gods coming into view," Mera said. "What else could you think of such a thing if you were them?"

"Exactly," Alex said. "The size and complexity of the vessels would have given the Taíno great pause. They would have seen the people on the ships as spiritual beings. It's why Columbus and his men were welcomed with such excitement and without any fear or resistance."

"Who knew chandeliers were so iconic," Phoebe said, smiling.

"Perhaps someday you can all come to the house and see the ones hanging there," Alex said.

"Sounds like fun," Phoebe said. "The house sounds amazing."

"Yes, that would be lovely," Mera agreed.

Alex went to the bar and reached under the shelf in the back.

"I have cigars I have been saving for some time," Alex said. "When I heard you were coming, I knew exactly who I had been saving them for. Shall we go out back for a smoke?"

"I think I'll pass," Mera said.

"Same for me," Phoebe added.

"We can stay inside while the men smoke cigars," Delia said. "If you are interested, I can show you some more of Alex's work and some of mine also."

"Sounds perfect," Phoebe said, and Mera nodded her approval too.

"Come with me, Amigos," Alex said as he led the way outside into the small backyard. "These cigars are amazing, and I can't wait to share."

There was a breeze in the back yard, masking the street noise. Several banana trees, heavy with bananas, hung over the patio. Julian paid particular attention to the smells and the light bathing the small rectangular area. There was a small table with four chairs in the corner to the left of the back door, and in the center of the table was a large ashtray with the remains of a cigar and some ashes.

Alex handed Julian and me a long, corona cigar. They were a brand we hadn't heard of.

Alex produced a cutter and lighter from his front pocket and handed them to me.

I cut and lit the cigar and passed the lighter and cutter on to Julian. I took a deep draw and held the smoke in my mouth. I was slowly exhaling, paying close attention to the smell and taste.

"This has a great flavor, Alex," I said. "I taste maple with a finish of coffee beans and maybe some cinnamon. It's very nice."

Julian had cut and lit his cigar and agreed with my assessment.

"I'm glad you like them," Alex said. "Here, try them with the Matusalem. I think you will find it quite complimentary."

Alex was right. The rum was an excellent pairing, and we sat quietly for a few minutes. The night was pleasant, with a slight breeze to compliment the taste of the rum and cigars. The cicadas were singing, and the bananas, hanging in long bunches on the banana trees with their fingers gathered into hands, were cascading down and ending in the bract with the male bud showing a beautiful, dark red color. *So perfectly sub-tropical*, Julian thought, *with its broad leaves and tender trunk.*

Julian knew this was his opportunity to speak to Alex about the favor. He also knew his close study of the banana trees was his way of stalling. After a couple of minutes, during which he had been unusually quiet, Alex spoke:

"Julian, I was working earlier today in Mariel. I felt my grandmother's presence. It was the strongest I had felt her in some time. I always use her for inspiration, but today, it was different. She was close, as if she was trying to tell me something. The connection to the work was stronger than it usually is. I slipped into a trance, as I was carving the image I saw in my mind. I had her voice in my head."

Julian felt a chill. Alex often talked about his grandmother and how much he loved and missed her. He was not a firm believer in communicating with the other side, so to hear him speak like this seemed more than a coincidence.

Whether this was a coincidence or not, Julian knew this was his chance to talk to Alex about his plans and how he needed Alex's help.

"Amigo," Julian said. "There is something I want to ask you. It's a favor, and it's a big one."

"You can ask me anything," Alex said. "And I will be happy to do it for you."

"It's about the house in Mariel," Julian said. "I'd like to borrow it this Saturday."

"Wait," I said. "So, you're not leaving with us on Friday?"

"No, Max," Julian said. "After talking with Caridad, I realized she could help me. She has had a premonition—a vision of my being here, including her involvement."

"Whatever it is you need, you know you are welcome to it," Alex said. "Maybe this is what my grandmother was trying to tell me. Maybe she was informing me about your using the house."

"Maybe," Julian said. "The next part may be the hardest for you to accept. I want to use it for an ancient Taíno ritual."

"Ah, I see," Alex said. "What kind of ritual did you have in mind?" He asked.

"It's called *Areyto*," Julian said. "It's a communion with the dead. It facilitates a visit with those on the other side. I know you are not a believer, but I hope you can help me."

"Of course," Alex said. "*Areyto* is an ancient word and an ancient custom. You know I will do whatever it is you need."

Alex's permission and offer to help did not come with his usual energy and excitement, and Julian felt bad.

"Alex, I know this is a huge favor," Julian said.

"I must admit you have surprised me with this idea," Alex said. "But I have to say, the house is the perfect place for this. The *Areyto* is not known to many people. It is amazing that you found someone who can help you. You know this kind of thing is dangerous, right?"

"Yes, I have heard much can go wrong," Julian said. "But I am willing to take the chance."

"Can we slow this down a little?" I asked. "Julian, how and when will you tell Phoebe and Mera? We have one more day of the conference and telling them now will worry them a lot. I know because it has put a huge worry on me."

"I know," Julian said. "But I can't make it happen any other way. I will miss my chance if I leave with the three of you on Friday. There is no guarantee that I can return and make the arrangements again."

I knew he was right. Travel to and from Cuba was always subject to change, depending on who was in power and which way the political winds were blowing. I took a long draw on my cigar and sipped some of the Matusalem rum. The taste of the smoke and the burn from the rum gave me clarity about what Julian was doing. I looked at Alex and Julian and realized

Julian had solved the last piece of the puzzle. Thanks to Alex, the plan was set, and there wasn't anything I could do about it. Whatever this *Areyto* ceremony was, Julian assembled all the pieces to make it happen. Sitting on the small patio with these two friends and surrounded by the sights and smells of the island, I experienced a clarity of perspective and purpose. Whatever challenges he would face and whatever outcome Julian was looking for with this ancient ritual, I knew I would help. I knew I had to have faith that Julian would succeed in whatever he was trying to do.

"This is a very nice cigar," I said, looking at Alex and holding it aloft so everyone could see it.

"I'm glad you like it," Alex said. "It's a nice cigar."

"Nice," Julian said, smiling.

We looked at Julian and wondered if he knew what he was getting into.

"There is one last thing I must tell you," Julian said.

"I am listening," Alex said, looking a bit apprehensive.

"There was a black witch moth in Phoebe and Mera's apartment this afternoon," Julian said.

Alex was staring at Julian.

"They managed to guide it out an open window," Julian continued. "As far as I know, it didn't touch either of them."

"Now, you have dragged me deeper into your mystical world," Alex said. "Let's hope no one was touched. Encounters with moths are not something we need to introduce into this equation."

The ride back to the apartments with Jesús from Alex and Delia's house was filled with conversation about the evening. The only thing not discussed was the conversation in the back courtyard while smoking cigars.

Intuitively, Mera and Phoebe felt that they should leave it alone. They must have noticed that Julian's and my moods were very different when we returned to the house after the cigars. They both knew something of consequence had been discussed. I'm sure they also felt that Julian or I would tell them whatever they needed to know.

Julian stayed behind at the Elita to settle the fare with Jesús. He waited until we moved out of earshot and gave Jesús the news.

"Amigo, we have a location for Saturday," Julian said. "It is a house in Mariel that Alex uses as a studio. It is on the water, has a history of use as a studio, and is a sanctuary for Alex's grandmother."

"Is his grandmother alive?" Jesús asked.

"No, she is on the other side," Julian said. "But Alex feels her presence there, and for him to say such a thing means her presence is strong."

Julian handed Jesús the fare and a piece of paper with the address of the Mariel house.

"I will pass this along to Caridad," Jesús said. "She will be pleased to know you have found a suitable place."

Later that night, Alex and Delia were lying in bed. Delia could tell something was bothering him. Alex was only quiet when he was working, and for him to be so quiet now was a sign something was either bothering him or, as she hoped, he was trying to work out a composition or an image in his head.

"Why so quiet," she asked.

"When I was outside smoking with Julian and Max, Julian asked a favor," Alex said.

"A favor," Delia said. "What kind of a favor?"

Delia knew Alex would do whatever Julian asked, and the idea of Julian moving in with them flashed across her mind. For a moment, she was concerned.

"He wants to use the house in Mariel this Saturday," Alex said.

"Use the house? Whatever for?" Delia asked. "Don't they leave on Friday?"

"They were supposed to," Alex said. "Everyone but Julian is leaving, and he is staying."

"What does he want with the house?" Delia asked.

"He wants to perform a ceremony," Alex said. "He wants to perform an ancient ceremony only a few people on the island know how to perform. To do it, he needs a place close to the water."

"*Areyto*?" Delia asked.

"Yes," Alex said.

"Do Phoebe and Mera know about this?"

"No, Julian asked me not to talk about it when we came in from smoking the cigars. Max is upset about Julian's plans."

"As he should be," Delia said. "*Areyto* is not something to take lightly."

"I know," Alex said.

"Did you tell him the house sits on the site of an ancient Taíno village? And that the ceremonial stones are still present?" Delia asked.

"No, but I have promised him," Alex said, the regret thick in his voice.

"And you will keep your promise, of course," Delia said, stroking Alex's head. "Please promise me you will keep an eye on him. I'm afraid he doesn't know what he is getting into. The fact he will be performing this on a consecrated site means that if this thing were ever going to work, this would be one of the places where it could."

"I will be at the house on Saturday," Alex said. "I will make sure nothing terrible happens to our friend."

THURSDAY

To Hell
with
Hemingway

Julian proposed skipping the conference's morning sessions over breakfast, and I agreed. Looking at the schedule, the presentations seemed of little interest.

"Let's do our own thing this morning," Julian suggested to Phoebe and Mera as we entered the small living room on the 11th floor.

"What shall we do?" Phoebe asked.

"Jesús will be downstairs shortly," Julian said. "How about a trip to the National Museum of Fine Arts?"

"I would love to see the collection," Mera said.

The museum was located on Trocadero and Avenue Belgica. The collection was housed in an enormous modern space that took up the entire block. As we exited Jesús' taxi, Mera was impressed by the building and the adornments on the outside.

"What is that sculpture?" she asked, pointing to Rita Longa's marble sculpture *Form, Space, and Light*. It was standing at eye level on the front façade.

"Rita Longa was self-taught," Julian said. "She was fascinated by the Taíno people and their culture, so much so that she created twenty-five life-size sculptures depicting their daily lives. The pieces are gathered in a reconstructed Taíno village in Guama. Her statue of Hatuey has become iconic and symbolic of Hatuey beer."

"It's amazing how prevalent the Taíno culture and history are in Cuba," Phoebe said.

"The influence is everywhere," Julian said. "Most people don't realize how powerful the history is and how it permeates so much of the island's art and culture."

On a projecting balcony, Julian pointed to high above the entrance where Mateo Torriente Bécquer's cement abstract composition inspired by Afro-Cuban musical instruments looked down.

"Here's an example of a syncretized presentation," Julian said. "You can see the progression from the Taíno to the Afro-Cuban. When we get inside, you will see the results of the final syncretization with Christianity.

Julian pointed out the last features of the building's exterior: the four corners of its two lateral façades and the sculpture groups by Juan José Sicre, Teodoro Ramos Blanco, Alfredo Lozano, and Ernesto González.

"Sicre was one of three artists who introduced modern European art to Cuba," Julian continued. "The others were Victor Manuel and someone familiar to you, but you probably don't remember."

"Who?" Mera asked.

"Antonio Gattorno," Julian said. "Gattorno knew Hemingway. There is a picture of him on the back of *Pilar*. They are returning from fishing off the Morro in Havana. Let's walk through the courtyard, to the back, and upstairs. I think this will give you the best feel for the space."

We spent the next hour and a half touring the museum, covering all three floors under Julian's direction and tutelage. When we were done, I suggested we go downstairs for coffee.

"That will allow us to discuss what we've seen," I said.

Julian took orders, and I went with him to help carry the drinks. We returned in a few minutes with the coffee.

"We don't have long before we have to return to the Riviera to catch the bus to the Finca," I said. "We can sit for a few minutes, though."

"Julian, the art is amazing," Phoebe said.

"It is quite a collection, considering the resources they have to work with," Julian agreed. "They get a lot of cooperation from the artists who are still living and the government. The art is a priority, which is important given the limited resources on the island."

"Given the struggles you talked about, making a connection to the island and your heritage, do you ever wish you still lived here?" Mera asked.

Julian was surprised by the question—not that it wouldn't have been obvious, but by the timing.

"Sometimes," Julian said. "Sometimes, I feel like I am not getting the full benefit of the Cuban experience."

"We were talking about that the other night," I said.

"Yes, we were," Julian said. "It's not an easy question to answer."

"Are you thinking about moving back soon?" Phoebe asked.

"No," Julian said. "I don't see it happening anytime soon."

I looked at Julian and couldn't figure out if he was being evasive or if that was a true answer. I hoped it was a true answer. That would mean Julian had no intention of staying long-term.

"I don't want to speak for Mera," Phoebe said. "But many behind-the-scenes conversations are going on, and we wondered if you were planning a big change in your life."

"Something big?" Julian asked. He didn't want to give Phoebe any encouragement.

I knew Mera and Phoebe were suspicious of Julian's conversations with Caridad and the one he and I had with Alex. I didn't know where Julian was headed with his responses, so I tried to deflect.

"It might be fun to visit you in your new place in Havana," I said, smiling.

"Well, don't pack your bags yet," Julian said. "I think moving here would be quite risky."

"Risky, and we would miss you terribly," Phoebe said. "How would I get my art history and advice on what art to purchase?"

"Look at the time," Mera said before Julian could answer. "We should get going. By the time we get a taxi and return to the Riviera, we'll only have time for one drink with Julio before we catch the bus."

I didn't know Mera's motivation for ending the line of questioning, but I was happy she came to the rescue. As it turned out, her prediction was correct. When they returned to the hotel, there was only time for one drink. Julio served up the last mojito.

In the
Shade of the Ceiba

"Paradise, sanctuary, peace and tranquility, the aroma of flowers and the taste of tropical fruit, the hummingbirds arguing over nectar from the bell flowers hanging in bunches on the pergola at the back of the house, a bookshelf and an ancient typewriter, the view from the bedroom window where so much of the genius emerged, and the view from the dining room where art and books and the smell of Cuban cooking coalesce. But most importantly, the place where the Cuban people, smiling, laughing, and living, gave "Papa" the energy and freedom to be himself, to write, and ultimately to share stories with the world."

— Anonymous

"She wouldn't float, even if you could get her to Cojímar," I said as I stood on the platform with Julian, studying Hemingway's boat, *Pilar*. We are staring at the fighting chair made of Cuban mahogany and the ship's wheel, stamped with the words "Wheeler Shipyard" and "Brooklyn, N.Y." Her deck is painted a deep green, and her stern is a bright yellow. She is dark and dry in the shade, her seams separating, and her caulk is dry and brittle.

Pilar, once the master of the great Gulf Stream, now battles the relentless assault of dampness, heat, and wood-boring insects. With limited means, the Cuban artisans strive to preserve her, maintaining a semblance of the iconic vessel once moored off the Torreón de Cojímar. An ever-changing testament to a life in subtropical realms, she holds untold tales from the Marquesas to Havana's Morro, from Bimini to the Caribbean isles. She'd echo those who faced mighty fish in the Gulf Stream's depths if she could speak. In silence, she witnessed the stories' beginnings and endings. Now resting on the Finca Vigía grounds, her sea-born spirit lingers as a ghost in the Cuban air.

"I wouldn't put her right in the water," I said with a wry smile. "She needs to be hosed down and allowed to swell up enough to make a tight seal. That alone could take several weeks. Then I would put her in the water."

Julian considered this for a moment.

"She's no longer seaworthy," he says as he leans down to inspect the hull.

"Stop saying that," I say, smiling. "You're ruining my big dream."

I know there is no possibility *Pilar* will ever float again, but I keep the idea in mind to maintain hope about her future.

While the marlin still run deep in the Gulf Stream unrequited in their search for *Pilar*, her days of hunting them are over. Even so, Julian and I feel the connection. These adventures inform every inch of her.

"I can see why your father loved working here," I said after a few minutes had passed.

"He did love it here," Julian said. "He was very protective of 'Papa' Hemingway and loved this house and property. Of course, Papa loved this place as well. He did some of his best work here."

Walking west, the tower Mary Hemingway built stands as a sentinel overlooking the main house. Never used for its intended purpose, it's a reminder of how deliberate Hemingway's writing was and how fragile it is to find a space to write.

Pilar is barely visible from this vantage point. I make one last attempt to look past the pool, and I can see her shape as we make the final turn toward the steps that lead up to the house. We slowly walk up the steps to the bedroom where Hemingway did almost all his writing in Cuba. It's the space Papa appropriated, not the space Mary tried to coax him into using.

Descending the eight stairs at the front of the house, we gaze back at the entrance, acknowledging the legacy of Julian's father. Julian's enduring tribute, the collaborative book, binds them across generations with stories spun in the shadows of the Ceiba tree. Although Julian never met Papa, the narratives shared by Ramón weave another thread, a lasting tribute from son to father.

Julian takes one last look at the house. He is thinking about his father and his father's life at the Finca. He wonders if he is seeing the house for the last time and if he is about to become one of the ghosts.

The Cathedral

Dinner the last night was at a small restaurant in Old Havana. I found it by chance down an alley off the Plaza de la Cathedral after talking Julian out of the pizza place around the corner. The host tried to talk us into eating outside, but the weather was too hot.

Once inside, the seating was cramped, but the air-conditioning worked, and that was all that mattered. The chairs and tables looked like something from the 1950s. To the rear, a high bar hid the kitchen and acted as the prep counter. The air-conditioner made a loud, whirring noise, but no one was bothered by it as long as it produced cold air.

"They have wi-fi. The server wants to know if we want the password," Julian said.

Everyone answered with a resounding no.

"Drinks?" Julian asked.

"I'd like a Mojito," I said.

"Same for me," Mera added.

"The waitress is bragging on the frozen daiquiris," Julian said.

"Ok, I'll have one of those," Phoebe said, smiling. "It should be perfect on this hot evening."

Julian ordered two mojitos and two frozen daiquiris. The server went off to get the drinks while they looked at the menu.

"What to eat on the last night seems so important," Phoebe said.

"I was thinking the same thing," Mera added.

"You can't go wrong with the lobster," I said.

Julian agreed with a nod. "I'm having the lobster," he said.

The server returned with the drinks. The mojitos looked average size, but Phoebe and Julian's frozen daiquiris were enormous, sitting in a giant stemmed glass and dripping over the sides. They were a rainbow-colored mountain of icy, frozen drink.

"Is that going to be enough for you?" I asked.

"I think so," Phoebe responded. "But I expect everyone to take a sip. There's no way I can drink this entire thing and make my way back to our apartment."

"Oh, come on, Phoebe," Julian said. "I know you. You can handle that drink. I have faith in you. Besides, I ordered the same thing and will drink mine; I promise."

Phoebe smiled and took a sip. "It is delicious."

The server asked for their orders, and everyone decided on the lobster.

The mood around the table was somber, and Julian was the first to speak after the drinks had arrived and the orders had been taken.

"Here's to Havana and the Hemingway conference," he said.

"Here-here," Phoebe said.

"I can't believe this trip is about to end," Mera added.

"Amigo," I said, lifting my glass. "We should have our last night ritual, don't you think?"

Julian smiled and lifted his glass. "Go ahead, Amigo, you always start."

I looked around the table. "When Julian and I bring groups to tour Havana on the last night, we always share a toast and ask everyone to participate. Phoebe, you are familiar with this. We haven't exactly been touring the two of you around, but Julian is being nice enough to indulge me."

Julian was smiling. "Go ahead and get to it," he said.

"Amigo," I said formally and in an official voice. "A famous writer once said, 'A writer should write what he has to say and not speak it.' Nevertheless, on this last night, I would like everyone around the table to share their most precious memory or experience from this visit. There is no order. You can start talking whenever you think you have something you want to share."

Phoebe and Mera looked at Max, both with pained expressions.

"What," I said. "It's a tradition."

"Ok," Phoebe said. "I'll start." She paused for a moment as she tried to gather her thoughts. "The paradoxes are striking," she said as she relived the moments. "When you're walking into what appears to be an abandoned building to find artists creating amazing works of art, the art itself rising from bits of cardboard, string, and paint. When you discover a Paladar in the worst-looking neighborhood in the worst-looking building, go through the narrow doors to find a sleek modern motif and a fantastic menu. Chefs create excellent meals from scratch with whatever they have available, using a farm-to-table model, not because it's fashionable but because they have no other choice. The thrill of finding what looks like a gutted building in a burned-out neighborhood, entering and finding beautiful young dancers."

"For me, it's the sounds and smells and the light. My God, the light," Mera said with a look of disbelief and admiration. "It plays off the buildings, the flora, and the people, many of them created from this impossible palette of tans and browns. I'm reminded of what the poet Nicolas Guillen said in 1972:—"Cuba's soul is *Mestizo*—half breed—and it is from the soul, not the skin, that we derive our definite color. Someday, it will be called 'Cuban Color.' Spain has come here, the English, Africans, not all by choice, and the Asians, the rest of the Caribbean, and, of course, the United States. No one gets the upper hand. The Cubans win. They have always won, first inventing themselves and then taking a little piece of what's right about the cultures, the cuisines, and the art of the so-called *discoverers*."

"One other thing I learned on this trip is that it doesn't take copious amounts of food, 250 cable channels, and 24-hour wi-fi, internet, and cell phone connectivity to enjoy life," Phoebe added. "Cuba's emergence will be so complicated that it's hard to know what to wish for the Cuban people. I suppose the best of what the rest of the world has to offer without the worst it has to offer. Of course, it won't turn out that way."

"In the end," I said. "As I see some of the worst decay in what has been called the Paris of the Caribbean, I feel a tendency to romanticize the lives of the Cuban people. Much of Havana looks like the leftover set from a disaster movie, yet the Cubans smile, move, play, dance, and create. But amid this paradoxical sensory excess, the struggles are always there, transcending generations and the memories of the oldest witnesses of the revolution and what was before the revolution. The beggars, young and old, and the street performers are a constant reminder that the Cuban reality is not fun and games but a fight for survival waged with a twenty-dollar-a-month stipend and food coupon books. These facts add a unique gloss to the experience, and I feel a level of guilt. The sense of knowing it will all change one day, with the best and worst of the revolution overtaken by the twenty-first century, tempers but cannot erase my sense of luck, timing, and yes, guilt at having seen it before the change and knowing these will always be cherished memories."

"Julian," I said. "You have been quiet."

Julian looked pensive as he glanced at each us. "Even now, after sixty years of change wrought by the current regime, it's not hard to see what Hemingway loved about Cuba and its people and why it broke his heart to leave. Whatever happens next will not be easy. There will be hard choices and harder sacrifices. Here's hoping the Cubans win again in whatever transition comes their way. They deserve better, and they deserve to write their future."

"I know you have a broken heart about this, Julian," I said.

"Max, I know you remember. It's the same outcome every time we bring a group to Cuba. Every day, at least one person in our group cries. Sometimes for the sheer joy of the experience and sometimes for the sheer sadness."

"I wouldn't trade this week for anything," I said. "Yet, I would trade everything to bring the Cuban people into the twenty-first century in a thoughtful, sane way. It is difficult to walk through the streets of Old Havana and not be conflicted by sadness for the way it is and about the fact that there will inevitably be change. It's the knowing that change will be both good and bad that brings the sadness."

Phoebe put her hand on top of Julian's. "The contradictions and paradoxes are overwhelming," she said as she looked at him, smiling and feeling sad. "Cubans seem wise beyond all reason and yet naive, full of life, and yet deprived in many important ways, surrounded by an abundance of spirit and creativity and yet isolated like no other civilized people on the planet. The Cuban reality defies understanding, and the way forward is impossibly complicated, but if anyone can do it, the Cubans can."

Julian smiled at Phoebe. Everyone at the table knew how important the last four days had been. They settled their bill, picked up their belongings, and walked out into the alley toward the Plaza de la Cathedral and an uncertain future set-in motion by Julian and the plans he had made.

Life in Full View

"I know it's warm, but I feel like walking," Julian said. "Maybe we can work off some of that dinner."

"Yes," Mera said. "A walk sounds wonderful."

Walking along San Ignacio toward Obispo, the doors and windows of the apartments are open, and the families are in full view.

Julian walked ahead, and Mera noticed as he passed that the people inside had stopped what they were doing and looked at him. Night had fallen, but it was still warm and muggy. The sounds on the street had shifted as families gathered in their homes and apartments to eat dinner, chat with neighbors, and sit in their window seats watching people walk by.

The cobblestones felt hard and unfriendly under her feet, and Mera realized, in Old Havana, that the streets had a way of keeping you connected to the island. The sights, sounds, and smells were a tableau of Old Havana and the people living there.

Daily life played out as if it had all been staged. The smell of food was intoxicating, even though they had just eaten. The children were spilling into the street, playing games or running around, inventing their fun. Mera wondered what they did with themselves all evening without the opportunities and distractions her kids had. They seemed happy and content to be doing what they were doing. *Kids are kids,* she thought. *They will find a way to entertain themselves.*

"Life in full view," Mera said. "How amazing."

"It has been like this almost since the founding of Havana," I said. "In Old Havana, there has always been this openness but still keeping a sense of privacy."

When she came to an open window, she was thinking about the children and noticed a woman sitting inside. The woman was dressed in all white and wearing a turban. A few moments before, Mera saw Julian walking by. He had turned and looked inside, giving a slight nod to the woman as she sat and stared out at the street. As Mera passed, the woman smiled and showed several gold teeth. At first, she thought it was Caridad, but she realized it wasn't when she looked closer. As she looked into the small room, her eyes met the woman's, and they seemed frozen at that moment. Mera had a brief sense of recognition, but it passed as quickly as it had come, and she moved past the window, and the woman moved out of sight.

"Did you see that woman?" Mera asked Phoebe.

"Yes. Did she remind you of Caridad?" Phoebe asked.

"Yes, she did. Instantly, I thought of Caridad, but then I realized it wasn't her," Mera said.

"Are you carrying your ring?" Phoebe asked.

"Yes, I am," Mera sheepishly answered. It hasn't been out of my possession since Caridad gave it to me."

"Mine either," Phoebe said. "I intend to follow her instructions, even though I have no idea why."

The women smiled at each other. Phoebe looked toward Julian. "He knows," she said.

"I bet he does, too," Mera answered. "We should ask him."

"I'm not sure I want to know," Phoebe said.

Julian and I had gone ahead, and Phoebe and Mera slowly made their way along San Ignacio toward Plaza de Armas and Obispo Street beyond.

"Those two are headed to the Ambos Mundos," Phoebe said.

"No doubt," Mera answered. "They have their agenda," she said, smiling.

Phoebe noticed a small shop as the men separated from the women.

"Do you mind if I go in?" she asked Mera.

"No, not at all," Mera said. "I'll walk in with you."

It was a beautiful, eclectic shop, and the two women were exploring all the offerings. Phoebe was particularly interested in a small sculpture of a fish made from recycled glass and wood.

"I'm going to walk ahead," Mera said. "We can catch up at the Ambos Mundos.

"I think I'm going to buy this piece," Phoebe said. "But I shouldn't be too long."

"Take your time," Mera said.

Mera left the store down the street and headed south toward Obispo.

As she moved closer to the Ambos Mundos, she heard a piano playing somewhere in front of her. She stopped for a moment to listen to the haunting sound.

It's a song she's heard before but can't quite remember the composer. The melody is sad and makes her think of Paris. Why does everything go back to Paris? She believes the music is coming from the left, but she's not sure where it's coming from, especially with how the streets and buildings are situated. It could be coming from any direction. She listens for a moment more and then continues toward the hotel. As she gets closer, she realizes the music comes from the Ambos Mundos.

Blue Night

Walking into the Ambos Mundos hotel lobby, Mera is transported to the 1930s. With no modern amenities, the space feels frozen in time. The piano is positioned to the right of the entrance, and an old man is playing a timeless, classic Cuban standard firmly embedded in the turn of the last century. The haunting melody of "Noche Azul," by Lecuona, drifts up from the ancient instrument and fills the lobby with its sweet melancholy sound. She wouldn't be surprised to see Ernest Hemingway seated at the bar.

She sees Julian and me sitting at a table to the left of the entrance, sipping dark rum neatly and smoking cigars.

"Well, hello," I say, spotting her in the doorway. "Let me get you a drink, and you can tell us what you've been up to."

"I would love a drink," Mera said.

I walked to the bar and ordered three mojitos.

We sat and talked for a while, sipping our drinks and listening to the old man play the piano. As odd as it seemed, it wasn't hard to imagine being back in Paris.

"There you are," Phoebe said as she walked into the hotel lobby and over to the table.

We had just finished our drinks, so the conversation turned to whether to stay at the Ambos Mundos or take a walk and explore.

"I think I'd like to keep moving," Mera said.

"Let's walk down Obispo toward the Floridita," Julian said. If we see something interesting, we can stop and investigate."

Julian settled the tab at the bar, and we headed west down Obispo toward the Floridita.

The party atmosphere was in full swing on Obispo, and we were surrounded by music.

"I never get tired of this," Phoebe said.

Julian and Phoebe walked ahead, and I followed along behind with Mera.

Costumed dancers moved past us, headed west, undulating in rhythm with the cadence of the claves, bongos, and maracas.

The Affection I Have for You

Julian and Phoebe were in front of the Hotel Florida, admiring the iconic statue of the dancer in the lobby as they waited for Mera and me to catch up.

"There's a famous nightclub in here, in the back," Julian said as we approached. "If anyone is interested."

"Let's go in," I said. "It sounds interesting."

We walked through the lobby and into the nightclub. The band was finishing up a break and it didn't take them long to regroup and start playing. The music was decidedly Cuban, and as people began to dance, the lights dimmed, and the room turned a deep red.

I found a table and motioned to Julian and Mera. Phoebe had disappeared into the crowd and was nowhere to be seen.

"This table has a nice view of the band," I said.

They nodded, and I realized they had no intention of sitting as they walked onto the dance floor, easing into the song's rhythm.

Phoebe walked up with a bottle of Havana Club and four glasses.

"I thought you were lost," I said as she sat down and slid the bottle toward me.

"Well, if this is going to be a party, then we need some rum," she said.

I opened the bottle and handed it back to her.

"You do the honors," I said.

"My pleasure."

She poured four shot-sized portions of rum into the glasses, raised her glass, and smiled.

"Here's to us and the feeling that Havana brings to all of us," she said.

I smiled back as I watched Mera and Julian. They had moved into the middle of a group of people, enjoying the music and the dancing. They were entirely in their element.

"You know how you know when a moment is special?" I asked, looking at Phoebe, not expecting an answer. "When you realize it in the moment."

"I agree," Phoebe said, looking at me, sipping the rum.

"It doesn't happen that often, at least not for me," I said. I was bearing my soul and had to do it without eye contact to avoid losing my nerve.

"I think that's true for most people," Phoebe said.

"We are on the verge of something, and I can't put my finger on it," I said. "I can't shake the feeling that we are here, like this, together for the last time—a feeling like something is ending. Maybe it's too much rum and too much of the Old City, but I feel an ending. Do you feel it?"

"I have many questions for you and Julian," Phoebe said. "Mera and I have been left out of a meaningful conversation. Something is happening that we have no idea about."

I looked at Phoebe and realized I started a conversation I couldn't finish without breaking a promise to Julian.

"It will all come to an end and be something new," I said, feeling a sadness that I couldn't quite define but felt real and urgent.

I could see Phoebe felt the sadness, too.

The set's first song had ended, and the band started to play "Chan-Chan."

I watched Julian and Mera dancing in a close embrace that left no room between them. They were caught in the emotion of the music. The lyrics were sultry and inviting, and I knew them by heart. It wasn't poetry; it was the music that drove the song's emotion; that was how I liked it.

"From Alto Cedro, I'm going to Marcańe.
I arrive in Cueto I'm going to Mayarí.

The affection I have for you.
I can't deny it.
I get the babita.
I can't help It."

The lovers, Juanica and Chan-Chan, are headed to the beach to collect sand. The story suggests they are building a house together or maybe a life. Mera and Julian dipped and swirled. A life built on sand, I thought. It didn't sound like a promising idea.

"From Alto Cedro, I'm going to Marcańe.
I arrive in Cueto I'm going to Mayarí.

Juanica and Chan-Chan
Sand hovered in the sea.
How the jibe shook
Chan-Chan was sorry."

Julian is holding Mera tighter now. I can see the sand swirling. Who builds a house on sand, I thought. Then I remembered it was me. I took another sip of rum and looked at

Phoebe. She was looking at me and smiling. I thought she could probably read my mind.

> *"Clear the path of straws.*
> *That I want to sit*
> *In that trunk, I see*
> *And so, I can't get there."*

I can't get there. *This song is about me,* I thought to myself, half joking. My glass was empty, and Phoebe poured me another shot.

"They look good together," I said.

"Yes, they do," Phoebe said. She left it at that, not about to wade into a conversation with me about Mera. She had never been too sure about our relationship and wasn't about to start probing now.

"I think that's her happy place," I said. "At least one of them."

"It sure looks that way," Phoebe said, smiling.

I turned to watch the band, having seen enough of Julian and Mera.

"I'm going to find the restroom while those two are dancing," Phoebe said. She walked toward the back of the room, headed for the lobby.

After a few more moments, the music stopped, and Julian and Mera walked to the table and sat down.

"That was fun," Mera said, looking at me.

"Where's Phoebe?" Julian asked.

"She went to find the bathroom," I said.

"I wish she had waited for me," Mera said.

"I don't think she knew how long the music would last. She said she wanted to go while you two were still dancing."

Starry, Starry Night

Outside the nightclub door, Phoebe took a deep breath. She asked a man standing next to the entrance if he knew where the restrooms were.

"The closest bathrooms were outside to the left, in the pool area," he said.

"*Gracias.*"

It was a warm night with a cloudless sky. Couples were sitting on chaise lounges arranged around the pool.

Approaching the bathroom door, a woman sitting in a chair signaled Phoebe for a tip in exchange for a small piece of paper. Oh no, she thought, forgetting about the custom in Cuba where women distributed paper towels or toilet paper in exchange for a couple of CUCs.

"Please allow me," a voice behind her said.

Phoebe turned, recognizing the man who had given her directions a few moments ago.

"Thank you, but really, you shouldn't," Phoebe said. "I can go back and get some change from my friends."

"Señorita, it would be my honor to come to the aid of such a beautiful damsel in distress," the man said, smiling.

"Well, if you insist," she said, smiling back.

"What is your name?" Phoebe asked.

"My name is Fernando."

He handed two CUCs to the woman sitting in the chair.

"Thank you," Phoebe said.

"It is truly my pleasure," Fernando said.

Phoebe disappeared into the bathroom, hoping Fernando would be there when she came out. She felt a rush when she found him waiting for her.

"May I buy you a drink, Señorita?" Fernando asked. "It's a beautiful night, and you look beautiful in the moonlight. I can get the drinks and bring them out onto the patio. It is much quieter out here, and we can talk."

"That sounds very nice," Phoebe said. "I'll be over there." She pointed to two chairs on the other side of the pool.

"Perfect," Fernando said.

Phoebe walked to the other side of the pool and sat on one of the chairs. She wondered if Max, Mera, and Julian were missing her. Julian and Mera were probably still dancing, which meant Max was still pouting. He's a grown man, she thought; he can take care of himself.

Fernando returned with a bottle of Havana Club and two glasses.

"Is it ok if the rum is without ice?" he asked.

"Yes, I prefer it that way," Phoebe said.

"You probably won't believe this," Fernando said as he poured rum in the two glasses and handed one to Phoebe. "I am not usually this forward with women."

Phoebe was smiling at how awkward he was.

"Where did you learn to speak English?" she asked.

"I lived in Toronto for a time," Fernando said. "I left the island ten years ago and moved to Canada with my parents and two sisters, part of the far-flung Cuban diaspora. I couldn't live away from the island, so I moved back."

"Why did you leave?" Phoebe asked, even though she was pretty sure she knew the answer.

"I knew there was no future here. Young people feel it more intensely. Waiting for change goes on forever, and we are born, grow up, get old, and die, spending our lives staring at the Gulf Stream, at the horizon, and wanting what's on the other side. I was one of the lucky ones. I escaped, not on a rickety raft but with the proper papers. When I got older, my priorities changed, and the idea of moving back, even with the limited prospects, was too strong for me to ignore."

"I can't imagine having to make the choices you've made," Phoebe said.

"Thank you for understanding," Fernando said. "Most Americans don't think about it. For them, Cuba is the regime, and the regime needs to be punished."

"Indeed," Phoebe said.

"We have talked enough about sad things," Fernando said. "The night is too beautiful, and the moonlight makes you look like an angel. I prefer to know what angels think about as opposed to talking about the difficult politics of Cuba."

Only a handsome Cuban, holding a sip of rum in the middle of Old Havana, could pull off a line like that, Phoebe thought. She smiled at Fernando, remembering Julian's warnings about keeping her guard up. But she was sitting in an enclosed space, steps from the door to the hotel lobby with other couples nearby. She felt safe, and the attraction to Fernando was starting to build. He smelled faintly of cologne and cigars—not the smoke but the buttery, spicy scent of cigars. He was wearing a black guayabera with tan trousers. His hair was neatly trimmed, and he looked and acted like he was well enough off to travel back and forth between Toronto and Cuba. Phoebe had other questions, but she didn't want the conversation to start seeming like a job interview.

"Thank you for the rum," she said. "I don't think I thanked you yet."

"It is my pleasure to be in the company of such a beautiful woman and to provide the rum."

Fernando reached over and put his hand on Phoebe's leg.

This is the point of no return, she thought. Phoebe knew her reaction at this moment would set the course for whatever happened next.

Fernando was sitting on the chaise next to her. The chairs were close, so their knees touched. In a burst of optimism—no doubt reinforced by the rum—Fernando stood, swung around, and sat beside her.

He reached his hands up and put them behind Phoebe's neck, gently caressing the back of her head and sliding them down to the top of her shoulders. Then he leaned in and kissed her, probing with his tongue.

Phoebe tasted the rum. The way he smelled and tasted made her feel weak. They kissed for a long time, and there was never a point at which she wished he would stop. They came up for air, and he leaned in and kissed her again. This time, his hands found her hips and then moved lower, pulling her close so she could feel his excitement. She could feel her excitement, too.

Fernando leaned back and looked at her.

"Would you like to go back inside?" He asked.

It was not the question Phoebe was expecting. Her answer was unexpected as well.

"I think I would," she said as she stood and rushed toward the lobby doors.

When she reached the double doors to the hotel, she went through and headed to the nightclub without looking back.

You are such big talk, Phoebe thought to herself. *Here you are with your fantasy coming true, and you turn and run like a frightened child.*

She didn't know whether to be proud or embarrassed. She decided being embarrassed and alive was better than being proud and missing.

An Artist's Soul

Julian and Mera were dancing, and I was sipping rum, contemplating the future. It hadn't put me in a good mood.

"Has anyone seen Phoebe lately?" Mera asked as she and Julian approached the table.

"She went to the bathroom about 20 minutes ago," I said. "That was the last I saw of her."

"Should we be worried, Julian?" Mera asked. "Should I go look for her in the bathroom?"

"I doubt she's still in the bathroom," Julian said. "Maybe she found someone to talk to at the bar inside. There's one up near the entrance. Either way, I wouldn't be too worried."

Mera sat down beside me, gently touching my arm.

"I'm going to find the bathroom," Julian said. "I'll look for Phoebe."

The band started playing again—this time, it was more Buena Vista Social Club. I was staring into my glass, and I could sense Mera looking at me, trying to assess my mood.

"Do you think Phoebe is ok?" Mera asked.

"I think she's fine," I said. "She knows how to take care of herself."

"The dancing was fun," Mera said. "This is such a great band, and Julian is such a great dancer."

"He certainly is," I said, trying to sound sincere, not sarcastic.

She touched my arm again, and I did my best not to be sullen or angry. I didn't know what I was angry about. It was so typical of my moods. It took me a long time to figure out how my mind works. But understanding and controlling were two different things. There was so much to think about, and Julian's intentions were only part of it. I wanted to talk to Mera about it but promised Julian I'd keep quiet.

"Who do you think he's talking to?" Mera asked, pointing at Julian, who was now deep in conversation with someone at the bar.

"I don't know. He knows so many people in Cuba. I'm always amazed at how many people recognize him and want to say hello."

"He's amazing," Mera said.

"How so?" I asked. I knew I was on tender ground, mine and hers, but I couldn't help myself.

"I like the way he connects with people. He instinctively knows what they need the moment he meets them."

"An artist's soul," I said, smiling. I took a sip of rum, focusing on the burn as I swallowed.

"Yes, maybe that's it," Mera said. "It's communication on a different level. Not spoken and not physical but some other level."

My stomach was hurting, or maybe it was my heart. Julian wasn't going back with us in the morning, and I felt like knowing and not telling Mera and Phoebe was a betrayal. Telling them would be a betrayal of Julian. He hadn't come clean about his plans to stay, but it would be the last minute since we were leaving in the morning.

"One thing I can say for certain is there's never a dull moment with this group," I said.

Mera was looking at me, and I resisted asking what she was thinking.

"Do you ever wish you could live anywhere but where you live?" she asked. "I spend a lot of time doing that."

"I don't know," I said. "I wouldn't put it quite like that. I wish I had two lives: one familiar and predictable like the one back home and one like this—edgy and unpredictable. one where life is filled with excitement. Where days hold some mysteries and danger."

"Now, you want to be a secret agent?" Mera asked, smiling.

"Yes!" I said, smiling back. "Don't I look the part?"

"No," Mera said. "You don't look the part. You look like a nice guy with a tender heart and a quick wit. You look like someone a person could get to know and like. Someone a woman could get close to, bond with, and feel comfortable with. Someone who sees into a person's soul and doesn't use that information for evil, but for good."

"Careful," I said. "I'm going to get a big head."

Mera put her hand behind my head as if she would lean in and kiss me. I knew that wasn't what she was doing, but it relaxed me. She slowly released her hand and let it slide down my neck and onto my shoulder, resting for a few seconds until she pulled gently away and leaned back in her chair. She stared at me for a long time.

"I think that's why you and Julian are such good friends," she said. "You both understand having a human relationship on a different, more intimate level. It's not sexual but more about how you perceive it. It's about how you both perceive emotion, desire, and intent. I don't know how to say it, but that's what I feel. That's how I see the two of you existing. This other world is what you get, and most people don't. That's why I love both of you, and that's why Phoebe loves both of you."

"The two of you talked about this?" I asked.

"Yes, we talked about it."

"Well, thank you," I said. "That's one hell of a compliment."

"The fact that you take it as a compliment proves the point," Mera said.

Julian and Phoebe walked up, and Phoebe's appearance immediately struck Mera.

"Well, don't you look all flush," Mera said, smiling at Phoebe.

Phoebe glared at her, a look lost on me and Julian.

"We should probably go," I said. "We have an early morning wake-up to catch the flight out."

"What time should we leave the apartment?" Phoebe asked.

"Probably no later than 10 a.m.," Julian answered.

"What time is it now?" Mera asked. "I have completely lost track of the time."

"It's 1 a.m.," I said.

Julian paid the bill while I waited with Mera and Phoebe in the lobby. The four of us walked out onto Obispo toward Plaza de Armas. Obispo was quieter but not deserted. A few of the bars were still open, and people were strolling, talking, and enjoying what had turned out to be a lovely evening. Julian was walking in front, and I hurried to catch up.

"Do you think we will find a ride?" I asked.

"Shouldn't be a problem," he said. "If we can't find one waiting next to the Santa Isabel, we can start walking along the Malecón."

I glanced back and saw Mera and Phoebe had distanced themselves. They were deep in conversation, absentmindedly following along.

"I wonder what those two are talking about," I said.

Julian glanced back at Mera and Phoebe.

"One can only imagine," he said, smiling.

"Julian, when will you tell them you aren't leaving with us?" I asked.

"In the morning," Julian said.

"That sounds like a terrible plan," I said.

Julian spotted a taxi and waved. He looked back and pointed to the car, so Mera and Phoebe knew where they were headed.

"I don't think I will get any sleep tonight," I said.

"I don't think I will either," he said.

The ride back to the Elita was quiet except for some light banter between Julian and the driver.

I settled into the seat next to Mera and looked at the ocean. Dark and foreboding, I was thinking about the ninety miles, the horizon, and the glow of Key West. I was starting to have a bad feeling about Julian's plans. We passed the Hotel National with its imposing rock cliff and the cannons pointing toward the north. What if it were only sixty miles, or 40 or 30? What if you could see the glow of one city from the other? It was an unsolvable puzzle as to how it would change the dynamics. What a sad mess.

"I'm going to miss it," Mera said.

"What?" I asked.

"Havana," Mera said. "I'm going to miss Havana."

"You'll never shake it," Phoebe said. "Once you've been here, you can't shake it. You can't shake the people or the feeling that they live in some *bizarro* world created by the rest of us."

"None of it makes any sense," Mera said.

"You have no idea," I said. "You have no idea."

FRIADY

Homeward

Back in the apartment, Phoebe spent an hour talking about the chance she had taken to go outside on the pool deck. She talked about how exciting it was, how alive she felt, and how afraid she felt.

Mera listened, asking an occasional question to be sure she understood the depth of Phoebe's experience.

"You took a hell of a chance," Mera said, shaking her head.

"I know," Phoebe said. "I don't know what got into me. It's not like me to come on that way and encourage someone I just met to take liberties."

"Liberties," Mera said, rolling Phoebe's choice of words around in her head.

Phoebe looked at the small glass of rum Mera had poured. Like I need this, she thought, but the taste and feel of it going down was comforting.

"Ok, so 'liberties' maybe isn't the best way to describe what happened," Phoebe said, smiling.

"You are one crazy lady," Mera said. "Crazy and brave."

"Brave, hell," Phoebe said. "I was full of rum. I will look back on this and think I was crazy. What was I thinking?"

Mera said goodnight to Phoebe and went to her room. She wasn't hopeful about getting any sleep. *Too much to process*, she thought. The trip was coming to a close, and it didn't seem like a good place to end. There was too much unsaid between the four of them. The word unsettled came to mind. We are unsettled.

There was a thunderstorm in full bloom over the Gulf Stream. Mera saw the flashes of lightning as she climbed into bed. It took a long time for the thunder to arrive, and out of habit, she counted the seconds from the flash to the sound to make an approximation of how far away the storm was. Four seconds, four miles, Mera thought. Her father had given her that approximation when she was a little girl, and she had no idea if it was correct. She hadn't even questioned it until a few years ago, and even then, she didn't check its accuracy. Ever since her father died, she was thankful that the lightning and thunder made her think of him. She wanted him to be correct, and he was right as far as she was concerned.

Other storms couldn't be judged as to how close they were. Mera felt one coming as she thought about the evening and how Max and Julian had acted.

There was another flash ... one, two, three, four, five. The storm was moving away, Mera thought. The other storm was moving closer—the Max and Julian storm was coming closer.

There was one more flash, and Mera started counting. She would dream about her father and look forward to whatever those dreams bring. It always happened when there was a storm.

One, two, three, four ... that was her last conscious thought before she drifted off to sleep in the coolness of the air-conditioner and its comforting white noise.

Mera's dreams of her father were always the same. She was a small girl whose father had taken her to the zoo. It was a warm day, and the sky was clear. The zebras were extra friendly and reached down to take the small treats she and her father bought at the concession stand. It was the last time they were together before he died. She was never sad in the dream, and she was never sad when she awoke from the dream. It was why she loved thunderstorms late at night.

Sunrise

The sun was breaking the horizon on the eastern end of the island. El Yunqué was still clouded in a heavy mist, and El Morro, still guarding the entrance to Havana Harbor, had not yet seen its first rays.

The view out Mera's window showed a deep purple sky, interrupted by streaks of pink clouds running horizontally across the vast expanse of water to her north. The remnants of last night's offshore rains provided a show of color and light as they often did, being the first to catch the morning sunlight.

Mera had been awake for some time. Lying in bed, she was trying to sort out their days on the island. Her memories seemed pressed together as if there had been one long adventure not separated by night or day or being awake or asleep. She heard Phoebe stirring in the bedroom across the hall. The sun was brighter now, and it was time to get up and finish getting ready. Maricel would arrive soon with another giant breakfast. Neither Mera nor Phoebe had been successful at talking her out of bringing so much food.

As if on cue, there was a soft knock at the door, and before Mera could react, Maricel had let herself in.

"Good morning, Maricel," Mera said. "How are you doing this morning?"

"I am doing fine," Maricel said, "Except I am sad because this is your last day."

"We are sad too," Phoebe said as she appeared from her room.

Maricel carried her supplies into the kitchen, and before long, Mera and Phoebe sat down to enjoy their last breakfast on the island.

Into the Light

Julian and I arrived on the 11th floor as breakfast was finishing. When she opened the door, Mera looked at me like she knew something was wrong.

We sat on the couch while Phoebe and Mera finished getting ready and gathered their luggage at the front door.

"Are you guys all ready?" Phoebe asked.

"Our luggage is downstairs," Julian said.

"Go ahead, tell them," I said.

Julian shuffled around nervously on the couch. Mera and Phoebe were standing in front of him, looking anxious.

"What is it?" Phoebe asked.

Finally, Julian managed to say out loud what he had known for several days, maybe since before we came to Havana.

"I'm staying here in Havana," Julian said.

It was 9:30, and Jesús would arrive at 10 to take us to the airport. I got up and walked to the window, looking toward the Gulf Stream and listening to Julian as he tried to explain why he wasn't going back to Florida as planned. It wasn't going well.

"If you don't come now, how will you get home?" Mera asked.

"I am home, Mera. This was my home when I came into this world, and it is my home now," Julian said with a steady firmness.

"So, you're never coming back?" Phoebe asked.

For Mera and Phoebe, the idea of Julian staying behind was sudden; it hadn't been discussed during the trip, not even at dinner last night when we relived the four days we had spent at the conference and on the island. Mera and Phoebe looked at each other and then at me.

"Did you know about this?" Mera asked. Her voice sounded angry, but she looked more hurt than angry.

"I have known for a few days. Julian swore me to secrecy," I said.

"I don't understand, Julian," Phoebe said. "You have a life and family back home."

"My journey no longer goes through those places," Julian said with a look of sadness. "My parents are both gone. My sisters have their own lives, and my future has always been here on the island. I didn't realize it until the other day in Regla."

"What happened in Regla that could change your mind about your future?" Phoebe asked.

"I met a priestess. She and I had a long talk, and there are some things I want to explore with her. Things that have to do with my father and my mother."

Julian was careful not to mention Caridad's name, now was not the time to complicate things.

"So, you've been thinking about this for some time?" Mera asked.

"Yes," Julian said. "The black witch moth appeared; the last sign I needed to know I was doing the right thing."

"Christ, Julian!" Phoebe said. She was animated now and raising her voice. The anxiety and frustration were evident in her tone and on her face. "It was a moth. We had fun with the excitement and surprise it gave us. We all made jokes about it. It scared me, but after the first shock, we all made fun of it."

"I know," Julian said. "But in the context of everything else going on, it meant more to me than just a fun story."

"Everything else?" Phoebe asked. "What else? You haven't shared anything else with us. It's been frustrating to think something is going on with you, and you're not sharing."

"I know you both have been worried about me," Julian said. "But there are things I cannot share. Besides the moth thing, for you, it is a fun adventure. I'm sure you will never encounter another black witch moth for the rest of your life."

"Where will you stay?" Mera asked, trying to change the subject. "What are you going to do?"

"I will stay here for a while," Julian lied. He felt terrible about the lie, but everyone was upset enough with the news that he was staying. He also didn't want them to be worried about the fact that he had no idea where he was staying.

"I have a million questions," Phoebe said. "No doubt the reason you waited until the last minute to tell us."

"Yes, I won't lie to you," Julian said. "That was part of the reason. The other part was not knowing what I would do until yesterday."

"But you have been thinking about it for this trip, right?" Phoebe asked. "Maybe even longer?"

"Maybe longer," Julian said.

"I hate to jump in here," I said. "Because I know I'm already in deep trouble on this one, but Jesús is waiting downstairs to take us to the airport. We need to get going."

Phoebe and Mera glared at me.

"Let's get these bags downstairs," Julian said. "Max, can you help? I want to say goodbye to Maricel."

Maricel had been hiding in the kitchen. She had heard Julian mention her. When she heard her name, she walked out and over to Mera and Phoebe.

"I am so glad to have met both of you," Maricel said as she hugged Mera and Phoebe.

"We are going to miss you, Maricel," Phoebe said. "Thank you so much for everything."

Julian walked to where Maricel stood as Mera and Phoebe gathered their luggage. With my help, they headed for the door.

"I don't know what Caridad has told you," Julian said.

"Yayi hasn't told me anything," Maricel said. "I knew this day was coming sooner or later."

"Thank you," Julian said. "If I don't get to thank you tomorrow, I want to say it now."

"Whatever I can do for you, it is an honor," Maricel said. She watched as Julian walked to the door and left. He had a powerful presence. She could feel it, and she was frightened and excited at the same time.

Julian took the elevator to the fourth floor.

Where Do We Go from Here?

Julian walked into our apartment as I was gathering my luggage.

"Mera and Phoebe are downstairs with Jesús," I said. "Is there anything else I need to know?"

"Only that I'm sorry," Julian said.

"You have nothing to be sorry about, Amigo, Except for that black witch moth thing. Did you have to throw in the moth thing?" I asked.

Julian was smiling.

"It sounded good at the time," he said.

"Really? Supernatural moths?" I said.

"They weren't buying my explanation about meeting Caridad," Julian said. "I didn't want to get into the whole explanation of their connection to her, the dance and the ritual. It's not something I'm supposed to talk about anyway."

"Yeah, I get it," I said. "Still, I will be explaining that one for a while. Where are you headed from here?"

"I don't know," Julian said. "I can't stay here past tomorrow. I already asked, and it's rented."

"When will we see you again?" I asked.

"It's hard to say," he said. "I don't know how tomorrow is going to turn out. Depending on that, I guess we will see."

After a long moment, I said, "Please don't do anything stupid. We have a lot of work to do on this Hemingway thing, and besides, who the hell am I going to smoke cigars with?"

"I'll be careful, I promise," Julian said.

I walked over and hugged him. We were both crying.

"Please don't screw it up, you crazy Cuban," I said.

"Get out of here before you miss your flight," Julian said. "Or before I steal your cigars."

I picked up my bags and walked to the elevator. Jesús helped me load my luggage into the trunk when I reached the street. Everyone climbed in, with me sitting in front where Julian would typically be sitting. It didn't help anyone's mood.

This is going to be a long ride, I thought, glancing back for one last look at the Elita and one last look at my past. Everything was changing, and while I knew why, I didn't know how. That didn't matter. Julian was on a different path now. For how long, I didn't know. All I knew was it didn't feel right.

O'Reilly Street

Julian knew he couldn't stay in the apartment that now had so many memories turned sad by his friends' absence. He walked around aimlessly for ten or fifteen minutes, considering his options before finally packing his belongings, going downstairs, and standing at the curb looking for a taxi. Standing patiently, he pretended he was still thinking about where to spend the night. The truth was, he already knew where he was going. His destination had been settled when he started packing.

When he finally hailed a cab, he sat in the back seat. There was no one else to sit in the back, and that realization compounded his sadness. He told the driver to take him to the old city. The driver asked where he wanted to be dropped off, and Julian could no longer pretend he hadn't known his intended destination.

"Drop me at the Plaza de Armas, please, Amigo," Julian said.

"*Si,*" the driver said.

The car pulled away from the curb, and the driver, whose name Julian did not know, turned right at the first corner and then left, headed to the Malecón. The Gulf Stream had pushed offshore, and the water was a greenish blue up close to the sea wall. Looking north toward Key West, he thought about his conversation with Max a few days ago. So much of what they tried to do was still undone—the connection between Key West and Cuba, the mirage.

The taxi pulled into the turnoff at the Plaza. Julian asked the driver for the fare.

"10 CUCs, Amigo," he said.

Julian handed him 13 CUCs.

"What is your name," Julian asked.

"Eduardo," the driver answered.

"Have a great day, Eduardo," Julian said.

Standing at the eastern end of O'Reilly Street, he stopped to watch the tourists milling around the booksellers on the Plaza de Armas. He hesitated momentarily, unsure of the appropriateness of what he was about to do. Cutting through the crowd and the memories of his friends so thick now in this space, Julian walked west across the cobblestones.

He had no plan other than to walk up to Ileana's house. The house was near Compostela, between O'Reilly and Obispo. Julian liked the location because it was far enough away from the harbor to be quiet and not so busy.

As he approached the front door, his confidence in showing up unannounced started to wane. It was rude of him to show up this way, and he was feeling guilty knowing he had other alternatives. The problem was he desperately needed someone to talk to, and she was the perfect person. She was an artist, and they had gotten along well when Julian and Max stayed with her the last time. When he arrived at her front door, he stood in the doorway, backing himself into the slight indentation where the double door faced the street. He couldn't bring himself to knock, and he couldn't leave because now, he had nowhere else to go. Finally, he got the courage to knock tentatively on the front door. It seemed to take forever, but eventually he heard someone moving inside.

The Flight Out

In the desert
I saw a creature, naked, bestial,
Who, squatting upon the ground,
Held his heart in his hands,
And ate it.
I said, "Is it good, friend?"
"It is bitter-bitter," he answered.
"But I like it.
"Because it is bitter,
"And because it is my heart."

— *Stephen Crane*

The ride to the airport was quiet. I couldn't tell if Mera and Phoebe were mad at me or were too stunned to talk or ask questions. I couldn't shake the image of Julian standing in the apartment as I walked away or the thought that it would be a long time before I saw him again.

Jesús knew enough to stay quiet, too. In the back seat, Mera and Phoebe were talking in low whispers. I couldn't make out a word of it. I wasn't sure I wanted to.

José Martí Airport was as busy as usual, and without much conversation, the bags were unloaded and moved off the curb. Jesús hugged everyone but was clearly in no mood for conversation either. Everyone was crying. I gave him a big hug, the fare, and a tip.

"Take care of the big guy," I said.

"You know I will do my best," Jesús said.

We headed for the counter and the adventure of clearing customs for the flight back to Florida.

Ileana

"Who is it?" a woman's voice called out.

Julian recognized Ileana's voice. It sounded muffled and hesitant; hearing it lifted his mood.

"Hello, Ileana. It's Julian."

There was a pause, and then Julian heard several deadbolts slide, and the door eased open enough for her to peer out.

"Julian?" Ileana said with a look of disbelief and excitement.

She pushed the door open and stepped forward to hug him. Julian's knees were weak. Her touch and the scent of her perfume filled his senses, and the memory of his last stay flooded back.

"Please come in. What a pleasant surprise."

He had forgotten how beautiful she was. Her dark hair hung a little below shoulder length, the perfect complement to her dark eyes and caramel skin. Her smile was radiant, playful, warm, and mysterious. Julian smiled back and felt himself transported into Ileana's world, even before he could pull his suitcase off the stoop.

"I've been here several days," Julian said. "I was with friends attending the Hemingway Colloquium at the Riviera Hotel."

"Where did you stay? You could have stayed here," Ileana said, looking disappointed.

"I didn't think you had the room. Besides, we were close to the Riviera, and the taxi rides to the hotel were short and cheap."

His excuse sounded weak, and he was sorry he hadn't thought of staying with her. He knew she could use the extra money. The government constantly changes the rules, and having outside income is always welcome. He considered the added benefit of enjoying her company over the last few days. Of course, the opportunity to visit would have been limited with Mera, Max Phoebe, and the conference. It was best not to have stayed here until now, he thought.

"I need a room for a few nights," Julian said. "Do you have anything?"

"I do. We haven't had many tourists lately, so I have the perfect room for you. I think it's the one Max was in last time the two of you were here."

Julian pulled his suitcase into the foyer and followed Ileana upstairs.

"It has a balcony and a view of O'Reilly Street. I know you like to people-watch, so this will be perfect."

Julian placed his suitcase on the bed, turned, and hugged Ileana.

"Thank you so much. You have saved the day for me. I don't want to take up any more of your time. I'm going to take a shower and then find something to eat. Thank you again for letting me stay on such short notice."

"You know you're welcome any time," Ileana said. "And, if you think I'm going to let you wander off for dinner by yourself, you have another thing coming. I'll have Tia fix something, and you can have a relaxing evening here. I promise to be quiet and not bother you, at least not too much."

Ileana flashed a smile that was impossible to resist.

"I think that's too much trouble. You've already done me a great favor, and to put you out any further would be too much."

"It's my pleasure. Besides, if you can put up with me, I'll join you for dinner, and we can catch up. You can tell me what you're up to, and I can share my expanding musical career with you." Ileana was smiling, and Julian couldn't say no.

"Yes, of course, but now I am embarrassed. I haven't asked you about your music," he said, smiling back. "So, you win. I will be pleased to dine with you."

"Good. I'll let Marta know you're staying. Let's say 7:30. That should give both of us time to shower and meet downstairs in the dining room."

"I will see you at 7:30," Julian said. He had forgotten how charming and playful Ileana could be. He was starting to like this idea more by the minute.

The bedroom was small but clean and comfortable. It had a connecting, private bath, a luxury in the old homes converted into B&Bs. Julian unpacked and took a hot shower. The water felt good, and feeling clean and fresh was welcome. He dried and put on the white linen pants and *guayabera*. He knew it gave him the look of a Palo priest, but he wanted to feel comfortable, like himself.

Having a few minutes to spare, he pulled out his laptop and read some of the ideas he and Max had been pursuing. He made a mental note to email Max the information he had gathered but hadn't shared. He knew they were undoubtedly worried about him back in Florida. He didn't have the strength or courage to tell them what he was up to. If successful, there would be so many questions. He couldn't help that either. He knew it was the right thing. It was his choice, and he would see it to the end. Lost in his thoughts, he heard a slight knock at the door.

"Maestro, are you in there? You are late for our dinner date!"

Julian looked at his watch. It said 7:45. He jumped off the bed and walked the short distance to the door, pulling it open to see Ileana standing before him.

"Ileana, I am so sorry! I am the worst guest you have ever had. I was deep in thought and completely lost track of the time. Please accept my apologies." Julian felt awkward, like he needed to beg for forgiveness.

"Don't be silly," Ileana said. "It's only 7:45. You still have another 10 or 15 minutes before you're late by Cuban standards."

Julian looked at her, marveling at her graciousness and her hospitality.

"You are amazing," he said lamely.

"How so?" She said playfully.

"In every way," Julian said. "In every way." It sounded lamer when he repeated it, but he couldn't think of anything else. He smiled sheepishly and hoped the moment would pass quickly.

"Shall we?" Ileana said, motioning down the stairs. "And, by the way, you look very handsome in your all-white outfit. You look very priestly. Palo, right?"

"Ladies first," Julian said, ignoring the question. He followed Ileana down the stairs like a lost little puppy.

Ileana's aunt, Marta, cooked breakfast for the guests and prepared light hors d'oeuvres in the evening. There was one other room with guests, but they had left for the evening, so Julian and Ileana were alone.

The dining room table had been set, and the kitchen aromas promised a delicious meal. Julian smelled pork and black beans, but other seductive smells filled the room, and he was looking forward to the food and the conversation.

The dining room, an intimate space with dark mahogany furniture, featured delicate lace tablecloths and vintage china from the 1920s and 1930s, reminiscent of Alex and Delia's house. The sideboard, set with lace and family photos, displayed an ornate mantel clock ticking softly, creating a rhythmic undertone to the conversations.

Julian recognized Ileana as a young girl in one of the photos sitting on the sideboard. She was next to her father on a farm. He was holding the reins to a team of oxen, and Ileana was sitting on the small wagon attached to the team. She had a big smile and was wearing a straw, *guajiro* hat, typical of the style worn by the farmers in Cuba. There were rows of crops in the background, trailing off into the distance. Julian guessed her father had grown tobacco, but he had never asked.

Artwork and family photos adorned the walls, showcasing various original pieces from the nineteenth century to the present. Julian always admired the richness of Cuban art displayed in homes and restaurants, feeling regretful for not growing up surrounded by such a vibrant culture. He thought about how different his work might appear under the strong influence of Cuban creativity and energy.

"Please, sit here," Ileana said, motioning to the seat to the right of the head of the table.

Julian sat down, and Ileana seated herself across from him.

"Shouldn't you be seated at the head?" he asked.

"I want to get a good look at you. Something isn't right, and this way, I can keep a close eye on you when I ask my probing questions." Ileana was smiling. Julian couldn't tell if she was being playful or if he was, in fact, an open book.

"I will try not to disappoint," he said. "Although I can tell you, there isn't much to tell."

He was contemplating how he would dodge Ileana's questions when Marta walked in with drinks.

"Daiquiris!" Ileana said. "Or, more precisely, Papa Dobles. In your honor, Julian. I couldn't let the evening go by without a nod to Papa Hemingway."

"You have thought of everything," Julian said. "A double should do the trick."

"There are more where these came from, so drink up," Ileana said. "I hope you're hungry."

"I think you can tell I am not about to starve to death," Julian said. "But being hungry is never a problem for me. Besides, if I wasn't hungry when I came in, the smell of Marta's cooking has done the trick."

He took a sip of the cold and refreshing drink. He tasted the rum and the citrus, and his mouth reacted to the tartness of the grapefruit.

"How is it?" Ileana asked.

"It's wonderful," Julian said. "Marta is as good a bartender as she is a cook."

"I asked her to hold off on the meal and let us finish our drinks. I have wine I've been saving. I think it will go well with dinner, and I didn't want to rush the evening."

Ileana stood, moved to the head of the table, and was now sitting to Julian's left. As she settled into her new seat, he smelled her perfume.

"There, that's better. Now I can see you and know if you are telling the truth or pulling my leg," she said. "Tell me about your trip. You said it was a Hemingway colloquium?"

"Yes," Julian said. "That's why we were here last time."

"Yes, of course. How could I forget? And how is Maximilian?"

"He is fine. He would have sent his love if he knew I was coming to see you."

"Was he here with you this trip?"

"Yes, he and two other friends left to return to Florida this morning."

"See, there you go again," Ileana said. "You are being so mysterious. Why wouldn't Max have known you were coming here? I know staying over was spur of the moment, but it still begs the question."

Suddenly, Julian was beginning to regret coming to stay with Ileana. It seemed like such a great idea. She was talented and intelligent, had an eye for art, and was beautiful. What could go wrong? Now, he knew what could go wrong—she would become intensely interested in what he was doing.

"There are some things I wanted to do in Havana. The more I thought about the trip, and when I might return if I left this morning, the more I realized I should stay and get done what I want."

"I think that was wise," Ileana said. "The situation in Cuba is always fluid. You can never know when you might return once you leave."

"So, there you have it," Julian said. "Nothing more sinister or interesting than that."

"Except you still haven't told me what 'that' is. I'm sorry, Julian. I don't mean to pry; it's none of my business. But you look unsettled and distracted. The last time you were here, you had this serene quality. You were centered. Do you remember we talked about your religion and what it meant to you? Your father was mentoring you. I know your father passed over a year ago. I am guessing this has set you back on your spiritual journey."

"His death was a great loss to me."

"So, how do you move forward? I should ask, how have you moved forward?"

"Slowly," Julian said. "I look around Havana. I visited the Finca Vigía and saw what my father had always talked about. I saw the town and the people and wondered what it was like for him growing up. The people in the pueblo looked up to him. He was Papa's right-hand man. He was his closest Cuban confidant because Hemingway saw my father every day. Sometimes, Ramón was the first person he saw when he woke up. Hemingway did so much of his writing at the Finca. It was his home, and he loved living there. More importantly, he loved the people of the pueblo. There were so many things that gave him strength. The children gave him strength and enjoyment. Being able to walk the grounds uninterrupted was important to him. The smells and the sounds were all things that contributed to his writing. My father took his job seriously and knew the time Papa had to himself for writing was precious."

Ileana looked at Julian as he spoke. From conversations in the past, she knew he had a deep love for his father. This was more than the idea of a son looking up to and admiring his father. This was much more profound.

"Julian, the love is so obvious when you speak of your father. I don't hear you speak of your mother. Did you know your mother?"

Julian thought for a moment. It was true; he didn't speak much about his mother to Ileana or anyone. There was always talk of Ramón when he was in Cuba, and that was mostly in connection with Hemingway. Julian always bragged about his father, but his relationship with his mother was more private.

"You're right," Julian said. "And yes, I did know my mother. She raised me along with my brothers and sisters. I don't speak of her to many people. I have always felt lucky to have known and been raised by her. When she died, I was left with a great emptiness. It wasn't too long after my father died, and we could tell she was ready to go to him. The last time I saw her, she kissed me gently on my forehead and told me she loved me. I knew then that it was the last time I would see her."

There was a long pause. Julian took a sip of his drink, and Ileana did the same. She set her glass down and stared at one of the family photos on the wall.

"In our toughest moments, our souls are revealed, and sometimes we are left to know a mother through her children," Ileana said. "And so, it is. I have gotten to know a bit more of you by your gracious sharing. I have no doubt your mother was proud of you. I also know you were proud of her. Your face and the tone in your voice say everything."

"I think that's how boys feel," Julian said. "Especially boys like me, who require a lot of attention."

"You required a lot of attention?" Ileana asked. The heavy moment had passed, and Julian was thankful.

"Yes, I was a bit sickly as a young boy. I had scarlet fever and various other ailments. I was also pretty good at getting hurt. I was always falling and trying crazy things that put me in harm's way."

"It's hard to imagine that now, looking at you. You look so healthy, and you certainly grew up. You are over six feet tall."

"I am right at six feet tall."

Julian looked at his drink and realized it was empty. Ileana noticed, too, and called Marta.

"Tia, Julian needs a refill. I will come help."

"If it's ok with you, I think I'd like to switch to the wine," Julian said.

"Absolutely!"

Ileana got up from her seat and headed toward the kitchen. Julian followed her with his eyes, admiring the way she moved.

When she returned, she was carrying two bottles of French White Burgundy.

"I am going to let you do the honors," she said, handing Julian one of the bottles and the corkscrew.

"Of course."

Julian made quick work of the foil and the cork. He returned the bottle to Ileana, and she poured wine into two ornately decorated, cut glass glasses on the sideboard. Ileana walked back to the table and sat down at the head.

"Here's to us," she said. "Here's to a pleasant evening, a wonderful meal, and the joys of sharing. Here's to mothers who love their children."

They touched glasses, and Julian took a sip. It was a Mâconnaise wine, and he tasted the citrus and felt its coolness. He also tasted a bit of oak. Oak was unusual for the region, and he liked that there was a hint of it. It would be complicated to get French wine in Cuba. Julian knew Ileana must have been saving it for some special occasion.

"This is a nice wine, Ileana. Thank you for sharing."

"I brought it back the last time the orchestra traveled to France. It was a miracle that I managed to get the bottles through the Martí Airport without disappearing."

"I understand it's a tough gauntlet," Julian said. "My trouble always comes stateside. Max makes me carry the rum and cigars back to Florida. I usually have the most room in my suitcase. I always get pulled to the side in customs and asked a lot of questions. I assume because I'm Cuban."

"So, your story is Max makes you?" Ileana was smiling and shaking her head.

"That's the story I'm sticking with," Julian said, smiling back.

"Good luck with that," Ileana said. "If you think I'm going to believe that the two of you aren't in complete agreement on strategy with your schemes, then you are in for a surprise."

Julian took another sip of wine, focusing on the terroir. It tasted tart and clean on his tongue. Marta was in the kitchen preparing dinner. It wouldn't be long before the food was on the table.

He was thinking about Max and their friendship and schemes, as Ileana called them. All of that could end, and he would be responsible. Suddenly, he felt a profound sadness. He may never see his friends again. Max, Phoebe, Mera, and the hundreds of other people he had met as part of the Hemingway journey. How would he remember them? What would those experiences feel like? How would he cope if it all went to darkness?

"There you go again," Ileana said, breaking Julian out of his trance. "You were zoned out. What am I going to do with you?"

Before Julian could answer, Marta walked into the dining room with two plates. The black beans, white rice, and pork were piled high, and the plantains and yucca barely fit. The yucca was seasoned with garlic and combined with onions, seasoning, and olive oil. Marta set Julian's plate down in front of him.

"Thank you, Marta. This looks and smells amazing," Julian said, looking at the plate piled high with food.

Marta set Ileana's plate down in front of her. She walked over to the sideboard and picked up the wine, topping off Ileana's and Julian's glasses.

"I hope you enjoy it," Marta said.

"I'm sure I will," Julian answered.

"Thank you, Tia Marta!" Ileana said.

The meal was as delicious as it looked, and the conversation with Ileana was light. The pork was tender and full of garlic, oregano, and sweet basil. The beans had been cooked with onions and the same chunks of garlic, basil, and oregano, the difference being the cumin that made them taste like home. Julian kept the topic away from his plans on the island. Ileana seemed content, at least during dinner, to spend the time catching up. Julian talked extensively about what he and Max had been doing around the Hemingway project. He also spoke about his painting and the things that inspired him. He didn't realize this until he was explaining to Ileana how intertwined his painting was with the work he and Max were doing. Ileana talked about her music and the pleasure she gets from playing with the orchestra. The opportunity to travel was part of the advantage of being a musician in Cuba. It was the best way for Cubans to see the world, and she had been to Europe and Japan since she and Julian had last seen each other.

Before he knew it, the meal had ended, and Marta was offering dessert.

"Marta, the meal was delicious," Julian said as Marta entered the room.

"I'm glad you liked it. We have dessert if you have room."

"I think I will skip dessert, Marta, but thank you," Julian said. "I am trying to watch my figure."

Ileana also passed on dessert, and they leaned back in their seats to finish the last wine. At some point during the meal, they had moved to the second bottle, with Julian doing the honors of opening and pouring it.

Julian was looking at Ileana, illuminated by the room's candlelight and warmly lit lamps. She looked content and vulnerable in the soft glow, and he wished he could stay and admire her without speaking or moving. He wondered when she would pick up the subject of his future on the island, and he was prepared to take on the questions. His arrival was a considerable imposition on her, and he owed her an honest answer.

"That was a great meal, Ileana," he said. "I know what an imposition this was, and I want to apologize again for showing up unannounced."

"Julian, you are such a silly man. You know I couldn't be more pleased to see you. This has been such a pleasant evening, and I hope it isn't over. I have an idea," she said. "Let's go for a walk. I'm stuffed, and I think the exercise will do me good. Would you be up for that?"

"Yes, I would," Julian said. "I feel the same way. A walk sounds perfect."

"Wonderful. Let me change into something more comfortable for walking, and I will meet you back here in ten minutes."

Ileana stood up and walked to the stairway. She looked back and smiled.

"I will be here," Julian said.

Cadence

Julian sat alone in the dining room. The mantel clock sounded like a metronome, and he focused on its measured cadence. He stood and walked around the room, looking carefully at each family photo. There was the usual mix of poses, both individual and multi-generational. Ileana was included in all of them, apart from one portrait that Julian guessed was of her mother. As he leaned in to look closer, Ileana appeared at the bottom of the staircase.

"I see you have found my grandmother."

Julian was startled. She had changed into white slacks and a black halter top, and her hair was still hanging loose on her shoulders. He smiled when he saw her, and she smiled back.

"I didn't hear you coming," he said. "I would have guessed she was your mother; you look like her."

"I don't have any pictures of my mother. She wasn't around when I was growing up. My grandmother raised me. She and my father ran the farm."

"She looks tough, self-assured," Julian said, looking back at the photograph.

"She was, but she also had a big heart. I loved her very much. I was thinking about her when you were talking about your mother."

"I'm sorry if I brought up difficult memories," Julian said. "Not having your mother must have been hard."

Ileana motioned toward the front door. "We should go before it gets too late," she said,

"Yes, of course," Julian said. "I'm ready."

"Tia, we are leaving," Ileana called to her aunt. "We shouldn't be late."

The front door opened, and they walked onto the narrow street. It was 9:30, and the sun was set. A soft glow of streetlights illuminated the people walking in both directions. Julian always loved Havana at night. The streets had the usual sepia glow, and the people were all in a slower, more cheerful mood than during the day. They walked down Compostela and turned left onto Obispo. As they made the turn, Ileana came close, reached under Julian's left arm, and took his hand.

"I hope you don't mind," she said, looking up at him. "I am feeling close to you tonight."

Julian didn't speak. He took a deep breath and smiled at her. She smiled back, and he felt his body relax.

As they strolled down Obispo, they were surrounded by a vibrant mix of locals and tourists. The street fluctuated between narrow passages and wider expanses, transitioning from storefronts to government buildings and back to retail. Although most shops were closed, the night came alive with energy as bars and restaurants took center stage. Bands spilled onto the streets, claiming the territory surrendered by the vendors. Havana transformed in its nightly metamorphosis and being part of it felt like a gift. Anyone taking notice might mistake Julian and Ileana for a couple, given the natural connection expressed in their body language and the way they effortlessly walked together down the lively street.

"I never knew my mother," Ileana said as they approached the Hotel Florida. "She left when I was very young. My father said she didn't like life on the farm. It doesn't get any more cliché than that, does it?"

"Let me guess, you blamed yourself," Julian said as they approached the hotel's entrance. They were stopped now in full view of the statue of the dancer on the pedestal that occupied the main entrance. "Let's go in. I was thinking of Ambos Mundos for a drink, but this will be much quieter."

Julian's mind was full of memories from last night with his friends, the conversations echoing, and his feelings for them heavy on his mind. For a moment, he was somewhere else or at some other time.

"Are you ok?" Ileana asked.

"I'm fine," he said. "I was thinking about another time when I was here, and it brought back powerful memories."

"Julian, you are such a complicated and mysterious man," Ileana said.

"Don't forget confused," he said, smiling.

"I don't think you are ever confused," Ileana said. "You may think you are, but I think you know exactly who you are and where you are headed."

If only that were true, Julian thought.

They walked into the lobby and made their way to the bar. One other couple was sitting at the far end.

"I think I'd like a table," Ileana said.

Julian caught the attention of one of the bartenders, who followed them as they found a table in the corner.

"*Buenos Noches*," Julian said as the bartender approached. "Ileana, what would you like?"

"I would like rum," she said. "I think the Havana Club Especial if you have it, no ice.

"The same for me, *por favor*," Julian said.

Julian was looking at Ileana and trying to think of something clever and encouraging. For the second time that evening, he sensed strength and vulnerability, and he couldn't help but think of the photograph of Ileana's grandmother in the dining room.

"You do look so much like your grandmother," he said. "She must have been strong; you were lucky to have her."

"My father never got over my mother leaving. But I have to say I never felt like he blamed me or loved me any less for her having left."

"Look at you," Julian said. "You turned out fine. I know that's small comfort when you have lost someone and can't get them back."

"The truth is, I didn't want to live on the farm either," Ileana said, smiling. "I must be honest with myself and own the fact I left too. But I don't want to talk about me. It's ancient history. I'm more interested in what you are up to. You are staying a few extra nights to do something you feel compelled to do, and now it's time for you to come clean."

The drinks arrived, and Julian raised his glass to Ileana and took a sip. The rum tasted warm and sweet and warmed his throat. Rum always reminded him of his father. The color of dark rum and the way it tasted evoked the sugarcane and the mountains and the harvest Ramón was forced to take part in for two years as the price for his family getting permission to leave Cuba.

"I met a woman here on the island, in Regla, actually," Julian said. "It was a complicated roundabout way that I met her, but that's a story for another time. She has offered to help me on a journey to speak with my parents."

"I don't understand," Ileana said. "Both your parents are dead."

"There is an ancient ritual that can be performed to put a believer in touch with relatives on the other side," Julian said. "This ritual traces back in Cuba to the Taíno. It was performed for centuries before Columbus arrived, and all the Indigenous religious practices were coopted into the Christian religion under the threat of death. I am meeting her tomorrow. She has planned for the ritual. She claims to not only have the ability to gather and instruct the necessary participants but also to perform the ceremony."

"Julian, this all sounds a bit unbelievable. Are you sure this woman can be trusted?"

Ileana looked worried. She was unconvinced about the wisdom of trying something like Julian described.

"You say you have only known her for a day or two?" She asked.

"I know it's strange," Julian said. "I can't explain it. I feel like my father is trying to reach out to me, and he is trying to do it through her."

"What is this mysterious woman's name?"

"Her name is Caridad," Julian said. "She met my two friends, the ones I was here with, on their flight five days ago. The way it all happened was quite odd."

"Has she asked you for money?"

"No, she hasn't asked for anything other than to be a part of what I am asking her to arrange."

"Julian, I am afraid for you," Ileana said. "When you showed up at my door, I was so happy to see you. The fact is, I have thought a lot about you since you were here two years ago. I understand you feel you are on a spiritual path. Your father must have known you were special to have spent so much time with you, teaching you and passing his knowledge on to you. But this feels very dangerous."

"It is dangerous," Julian said. " With my father's passing, I have come to an impasse. I feel he needs me to help him cross to the other side. It's also my time to revisit who I am and choose who I want to be. My painting has always reflected who I think I am and the truth I find in the world. I believe the spirit world surrounds us. Images and energies unseen shape our reality. The challenge has always been capturing the urgency without sacrificing the beauty. I infuse the concept of Duende into everything I do—painting, writing, filmmaking, precisely because the world is filled with great beauty but also great tragedy. The Cuban diaspora wanders, searching for our place on the island, even if we never expect to inhabit that space physically. So, I am like every Cuban displaced from their spiritual home. How do we find our way back and connect to what is in our souls? The Palo religion gives me some answers to that question. I have to have the courage to take the path available to me. If I can reach my father and help him on his way, then I am willing to take the risk."

"They were your connection, weren't they," Ileana said. "They were your connection to the island. Your connection to who you are. Now they are both gone, and you don't know where to go from that loss."

"I hadn't thought of it that way, but I think you are right," Julian said. "My father and mother represented who we are and where we came from. I was too young when we left. I didn't have the memories they had. Hearing them talk about Cuba and the life we all had before we left was what kept me connected."

"Doesn't your work keep you connected?"

"My work is important to me, of course. But the work always came from my connection to my family. In particular, my parents were a great inspiration for me."

"Then you must find your way," Ileana said. "I know there are a lot of people who don't want to lose you. I count myself in that group."

"It's not my intention to get lost," Julian said, smiling. "This ritual isn't supposed to kill off the participant."

Ileana looked down at her glass and took the last sip of rum. Julian had been finished for some time.

"Would you like another?" He asked.

"I think I'd like to go home," Ileana said. "The rum was very nice, but one more would probably be more than I can handle."

Julian walked to the bar and paid the tab. Ileana followed him and waited at the lobby entrance until he finished paying. As he approached, Ileana took his arm and reached to hold his hand without asking. It felt natural. Julian was grateful for the support, and the closeness made him feel he would have the courage to do what he wanted tomorrow. They walked together through the lobby and to the front entrance.

"What do you think she is trying to do?" Ileana asked.

"Who?" Julian asked, looking around for a clue as to what Ileana was talking about.

"The dancer on the pedestal," Ileana said. She looks to me like she is trying to ward off evil."

"Hmm, that's an interesting interpretation," Julian said. "It looks to me like she is trying to conjure her parents."

"I don't think that's funny," Ileana said as she tried to stifle a smile.

It was late, and the walk back to Ileana's house took them past closed shops and restaurants. The bars were still open, the music played, and the patrons were partying with great energy and enthusiasm. The music and the dancing, which had spilled out onto Obispo Street earlier, were now in complete control. The congas and claves were setting the rhythm, and the street seemed to pulse.

Julian and Ileana were silent as they strolled back toward the house, lost in their thoughts.

As they passed one of the open-air parties, Ileana tugged Julian's arm. "Let's dance," she said.

The band played a salsa, and eight or ten other couples danced. Julian was hesitant, but he could see by the look on Ileana's face that resistance would be futile. He followed her into the crowd, and they started to dance. Julian felt his mood lift immediately, and Ileana smiled and moved as if she wanted to stay and dance all night.

"I thought you wanted to go home," Julian said teasingly when the second song started.

"You can't expect a Cuban girl to stroll past a salsa beat, can you?"

"I suppose not."

After two more songs, they decided to end the dancing.

"That was very nice," Ileana said. "Thank you for indulging me."

"It was my pleasure," Julian said.

They started back toward the house, walking arm-in-arm. Julian had become accustomed to her being close and knew he would miss it when they returned to the house, and the magic of Obispo ended.

At the front door, Ileana found her key and opened it. Standing in the entranceway, the moment became awkward as neither knew what to say.

Finally, Julian spoke.

"Ileana, it has been a wonderful evening. I can't tell you how grateful I am for the room, the meal, and, most importantly, the company. When I decided to barge in on you this way, I hoped that you would be gracious and understanding, and you were both of those things. More importantly, you were extremely intuitive about my state of mind and came to my rescue. I can't thank you enough."

"Julian, you know how fond I am of you. At least, I hope you know. I have had a wonderful evening, and your showing up has been a delightful surprise that I wouldn't trade for anything."

Julian leaned in and kissed Ileana on the cheek. She returned the gesture.

"I will see you in the morning," he said.

"I hope you get a good night's sleep, Julian. You will need your rest for tomorrow. Sleep tight."

Ileana turned and walked toward her room. Julian's eyes were glued to her; the evening had ended too quickly. He reluctantly turned and started up the stairs, moving slowly and hoping she would call him. There was only silence except for the ticking of the dining room clock as it sent itself and him into the future.

SATURDAY

Maricel

Maricel woke, unsure of the hour and with the room still in darkness. Listening to her cousins breathing beside her in rhythmic bliss, she was jealous of their lack of restlessness or worry. Focusing on the subtle cadence, she contemplated life's fragile exchange through breath—oxygen in, carbon dioxide out. The magic of mere existence hung in the air, sustained by the mundane act of breathing. Their breath conjured an unspoken reverence for the astonishing.

She slipped out of bed, gently padding to the bathroom. Jesús was picking her up, and he had a busy day ahead of him. After taking her to Yayí's, he would pick up Julian and take him to Mariel. She wanted to be dressed and ready to meet him before he knocked on the door.

She was spending the day at Caridad's house in preparation for the ceremony. The mental and physical preparation for the dance was specific and intense. Each step was required to make the dance effective and trying it at home was out of the question.

Maricel's mother knew she was leaving early to spend time with Caridad. She thought they were spending the day browsing shops in Old Havana, which she and Caridad did quite often, so her plans didn't raise any suspicions.

When Jesús arrived, Maricel was ready. She slipped quietly out the door to not wake anyone, opened the passenger-side door, and sat down.

"*Buenos días*," Jesús said as she entered the car.

"*Buenos días*," Maricel answered.

"You look a little sleepy and tired," Jesús said, smiling.

"Just drive, Jesús," Maricel said with an annoyed look.

Jesús continued to smile as he pulled away from the curb and headed to Caridad's house.

Sunrise

Julian awoke to the gentle strains of Ileana's violin, a familiar melody from his Baracoa childhood—a healing tune his mother once hummed during his bouts of sickness. It was a beautiful song, and her interpretation was tender and soothing. The music reminded him of the women in white, gracefully dancing the Orisha's rhythm, channeling spirits to tend to ailing boys. He imagined hearing the soft trilling of the bracelets and the ancient rings adorning the dancers' necks; it was a journey through the echoes of both past and future.

As dawn broke, Julian glimpsed a hummingbird, pausing on the balcony. Stepping to the double doors, he looked out onto the narrow street. The vendors were stirring, breathing life into the old city. Looking towards the Gulf Stream and the Malecón, he thought of the sculpture of the swordfish and mermaid dancing in front of the Riviera Hotel, remembering moments shared with his friends at the conference. He wondered if the Gulf Stream, so efficient at swallowing everything in its grasp, had swallowed the echoes of their conversations, erasing everything in the past. Even at this distance, he sensed the energy of the great purple river flowing silently to the east.

With the sunlight streaming into the room, he walked to the bed and undressed. The shower felt good as the water washed over him. When the hot water started to fade, he thought the other guests would be mad, so he quickly bathed and rinsed.

Jesús was picking him up, but he had time to go downstairs for breakfast and a visit with Ileana. He didn't know if he was losing his nerve or didn't want to leave her, but last night's visit had made leaving much harder.

Julian started downstairs, and Ileana heard him coming. She slowed the tempo and lowered the volume of the music in anticipation of seeing him. He thought about how beautiful the music sounded as he reached the bottom of the stairs and how excited he was to see her. No imagination could have conjured the image of beauty and grace that greeted him.

She was still in her nightgown, modest in its style but failing to hide her radiance. Julian caught himself staring for an embarrassingly long time as she finished the last few bars of the music.

"Good morning, sleepy head," she whispered.

"The sun is hardly up," he said. "How early does a person have to get up to not be considered a sleepy head?" feigning bruised feelings, he added, "Besides, I thought musicians stayed out late and slept in."

"It's an old habit," she said. "Once a farm girl, always a farm girl."

"The music is beautiful. Do you always play first thing in the morning?"

"Only when I'm happy."

"Someone as beautiful and talented as you should always be happy. It shouldn't be any other way."

"You are such a sweet talker," Ileana said sarcastically.

Her expression turned serious.

"That would be wonderful, wouldn't it? But we all know life never happens that way."

"No, it doesn't," Julian said.

Contemplating his past and future, Julian looked at Ileana, wondering about the mysteries of her life. He wasn't about to ask as he approached her, settling into a nearby chair. Sensing a subtle, more intimate shift in her demeanor, he wondered if it was real or merely his hopeful imagination. At that moment, he imagined a future of quiet mornings with this captivating woman, where easy conversation and her tender presence could ease the weight of past sorrows. The melody of her voice held the promise of relief, a solace for the pains, suffering, and regrets that lingered in the recesses of every life.

"I'll get you some coffee," she said.

"Where's Marta?" Julian asked.

"I gave her the morning off. Our other guests had an early flight back to the States and have already left for the airport. What time are you leaving?"

"The driver is picking me up around 11:30 this morning," Julian said.

"Well, that gives us some time to relax and talk," Ileana said, lifting herself from the chair to get coffee.

"With milk?" She called from the kitchen.

"No," Julian said. "I like it black."

He knew the coffee would come out strong, black, and sweetened with sugar until it looked like syrup. Ileana came back into the room carrying two small cups.

"I hope it tastes okay. I'm not the one who makes the coffee around here. I should have asked Marta to make some before she left."

"It tastes fine," he said.

"Well, that's a so-so review," she said.

"No, really, the coffee is great. You missed your calling. If we were back in the States, I could get you a job at Starbucks instantly," Julian said with a big smile.

Ileana smiled back.

"Should we move on from the coffee?" Ileana asked.

"I think that's a wonderful idea," Julian said. "Ileana, I had a wonderful time last night, and this morning feels just as perfect. I feel a connection to you, and I can't ignore it. Considering how little time we've spent together, I know it sounds too intense. Do you sense this, or am I coming off as desperate and needy?"

"We are here, now, you and me," she said.

Julian sensed a nervousness and hesitation in her voice.

"Yes, we are," Julian said. "It is so nice to be sitting here and enjoying your company and your coffee."

"Thank you, but that's not what I'm trying to say; I'm trying to say that I feel like this is a moment we won't ever get back. I don't know what I'm feeling, exactly, but it feels a little like desperation."

She paused for a moment.

"No, not desperation, but a connection, as you said. It's a connection I don't want to lose. I am moving slowly, keenly aware of the importance and weight of everything I'm saying."

Ileana struggled with her feelings and what she was trying to say. Julian couldn't trust his own emotions because of the journey he was facing. He nodded, feeling inadequate and clumsy about his reaction.

"I mean to say—I don't want you to go," Ileana said, with tears and a look of emotional and physical surrender.

Rising from her chair, she was suddenly on Julian's lap. Her movement was graceful and quick, and it seemed to him that she had no existence in the physical world.

She put her arms around his neck. He felt her breath warm on his cheek. She stroked his head and, in one fluid motion, leaned up and kissed him.

The way she smelled and tasted overwhelmed him. He wrapped his arms around her waist. In a lingering embrace, she leaned into him before taking his hand and guiding him out of the sitting room and into her bedroom.

Ileana loosened the neck of her gown, and it slid to the floor gracefully. Instead of feeling exposed, she felt free and safe. She reached down, loosed the cord around Julian's waist, and his linen pants fell to the floor. He helped with his shirt, and in an instant, they were both naked.

Julian gently lifted Ileana onto the bed, sliding in beside her. Holding her tightly, he kissed her again, and Ileana's body responded to the intimacy they were sharing. She shuddered once, then again, and then her body relaxed. His weight felt safe, and she wanted to stay in the moment for as long as possible. She listened to Julian's breathing, slow, deep, and steady. She could have listened to him forever.

Julian rolled onto his side and looked at her.

"Thank you for making me feel safe," Ileana said.

Julian thought for a moment about her use of the word.

"I was hoping for something a little more exciting, maybe a little sexier," he said, smiling, teasing.

"I can't think of anything sexier than feeling safe. It's what I love about you. It's what makes you sexy," Ileana said. "Well, one of the things."

She moved closer and put her arms around him. She felt the muscles ripple in his back and smelled the soap he had used in the shower earlier that morning.

They were quiet for a long time.

"When are you leaving?" Ileana finally asked.

"I have to go soon," Julian said.

"I know." She paused for a moment, struggling with the next question. "Will you be back?"

She asked the question, knowing it wasn't the time or the place, but there would be no other time or place. She heard the pleading tone in her voice and was sure Julian heard it, too. She turned away from him, and Julian moved close to her and put his arm across her waist. His chest pressed against her back, and she felt warm and reassuring breath on her neck. Ileana couldn't remember the last time she felt so connected to someone.

"I'm not sure," Julian said. "I don't know what's going to happen later, and I don't know what the outcome will be. No one has tried this in a very long time. My belongings are in the room. If something happens to me, if I don't return, throw everything away. There isn't anything of value."

Julian reached up and placed his hand on Ileana's right breast. As they lay there next to each other, she felt overwhelmed by the moment's intimacy and desperate to talk Julian out of what he was about to do.

"Aren't you afraid?"

"Yes."

"Then why do you want to do it?"

"I have to know."

"What do You have to know?" She asked again, even though she knew the answer.

"I must know if my father is safely on the other side."

"You're being so dramatic," Ileana said, trying not to sound harsh. "Everyone wants to know about the other side. What if there is no other side? What if this ritual doesn't take you there? What if it takes you there and you can't come back? What if nothing happens? Are you prepared for all these potential outcomes?"

"I think I am," Julian said. He knew when he said it that he was trying to sound surer than he was.

There was more silence. Ileana rolled over and looked at Julian, trying to decide what to say next.

"Sometimes, when playing music in the house, I feel transported to the other side. Do you ever feel that way with your painting? You talked about it last night."

"Sometimes," Julian said.

"But that's not communication, is it," Ileana said. "That's what you're looking for, and you can't get that with your painting."

"Yes, that's true," Julian said.

"And the dreams aren't enough?"

"In the dreams, my father asks for my help," Julian said. "That's why I feel so compelled to get closer to him through the ritual."

Ileana was feeling discouraged. She knew Julian had made up his mind about what he was going to do. She breathed a deep sigh.

"I have a bad feeling about this," she said. "But I know your mind is made up."

Julian looked at her, feeling a sense of foreboding and doubt. Was he being foolish? Was Ileana right? What if this journey left him stuck in the same place he feared his father was? What if it was some false promise, a useless exercise?

After a long silence, Julian rolled over and sat up. It was late, and Jesús would be there soon. He leaned over and kissed Ileana on the cheek. She reacted with a deep breath that sounded like surrender. The price of his actions had gone up, and the difficulties of sticking to his plan had increased in immeasurable personal and emotional ways.

He gathered his clothes and moved into the bathroom to get dressed. Looking at himself in the mirror, he wondered who he was seeing. He was feeling out of control, but events and actions were in motion, and his destiny, whatever it was, was now set.

Julian washed up and got dressed. He took one last look in the mirror, opened the bathroom door, and walked back into the bedroom. Ileana remained motionless. He stood momentarily looking at her, then walked out of the bedroom and headed to his room.

Standing at the double door, looking out onto O'Reilly Street, he spotted Jesús in the green Chevrolet. He straightened the room, set his bag in the corner so it would be out of the way, and walked slowly down the stairs.

Ileana met him at the bottom of the stairs wearing the white nightgown, and he could see she was crying.

"I want you to promise me you will be safe," she said. "I want you to promise me you will come back."

Julian looked at her. He tried to muster a smile, but his emotions betrayed him.

"I will do my best," he said. "I will see you tomorrow and tell you about my adventure."

Ileana reached up and put her hands on the back of his neck. She pulled him down and kissed him. Julian reached around and drew her close. He felt the energy rise inside him. He felt the love and hoped she felt it, too.

He opened the heavy front door, and the sunlight poured into the small foyer. He walked onto the street where Jesús was waiting. The door closed behind him, and he heard the rasping sounds of the deadbolts moving into place. He thought he heard the clock ticking in the dining room, but he knew it was his imagination. He realized now that there would be no ticking to take him into the future; he would have to do that alone.

Mariel

Julian and Jesús arrive at the house in Mariel an hour before sunset. Jesús pulls into the yard and turns off the engine. Julian reaches into his pocket for the fare, and Jesús waives him off.

"This one is on me, Amigo," he says. He looks at Julian and smiles. He knows this may be the last time he sees his new friend, but his fears about such things go unspoken.

As they walk toward the house, Julian hears people practicing inside as the bongos, tambours, and claves merge into the ancient rhythm used in the ceremony. It sounds similar to the classic rhumba beat but differs in crucial ways. He can't put his finger on it, but it feels more ominous.

There is a wide hallway running the length of the house, and as Julian enters, he sees the original chandeliers hanging in the rooms on either side of him. Graceful and delicate, they cast their amber glow, creating an ethereal ambiance reminiscent of the chandeliers in his paintings. Each room holds the original furniture and artwork, and he remembers the story of Angelita wandering through the house, mourning her lost adopted family. The energy in the house is palpable, and he understands why the surroundings nourish Alex's creativity.

Jesús stops at the first room on the left, and Julian continues toward the kitchen. The musicians, scattered throughout the house, tune their instruments, falling in sync, and the music adds to the dreamlike atmosphere.

Caridad arrives with Maricel and several other women. Maricel and the others stay at the front of the house, and Caridad continues down the hallway toward Julian. Looking calm and in control, she is dressed in white with a white turban, her bracelets, and shells making trilling sounds as she moves toward him. Julian is surprised he can hear her over the instruments.

"How are you doing?" Caridad asks when she reaches the kitchen.

"I'm fine," Julian answers. "A little nervous."

"I have a good feeling about this house," Caridad says. "Maricel has had a good day, and I am confident she is ready."

Caridad hands Julian an elongated porcelain container and a necklace made of cowry shells. The container has a delicate filigree edge. The top has a small round knob, and the outside of the container is painted with small figures, men and women, who are dancing. Julian recognizes the style as typical of the bone china found on many personal alters in Cuba.

"This is a cigar laced with cohoba powder," Caridad says. "Don't light it until I tell you. The shells are from Baracoa and have been in my family for generations. Please put them on and do not take them off."

Julian nods and leans down so Caridad can help him with the shells. He lifts the small lid of the box and peeks inside. The corona cigar rests in a cedar lining and is unmarked. The wrapper is dark, a Maduro, and suggests age. Even in the container, Julian can smell the tobacco with hints of leather and spices.

Alex, seated at the kitchen table, stands and greets Caridad, looking agitated.

"I hope this house suits your purpose," he says.

"The house is lovely," Caridad says. "There is great energy here. There is also history, some of which I sense is quite complicated."

"The house has been here a long time," Alex says. "And, yes, some of the history is complicated, as you say."

"Can we see out back?" Caridad asks.

"Of course."

Alex leads Caridad and Julian into the back yard, surrounded by mango trees. The land slopes gradually toward the shore, and the mango trees give way to mangroves that reach twenty feet into the water. The mangroves form a semicircle, and there is an opening with an unobstructed view to the sandy-bottom shallows that eventually transition to deeper water and then the Gulf Stream.

The concentric circles, gathered and placed by the Taíno hundreds of years before the Europeans arrived, are the backyard's main feature, and Caridad recognizes them immediately. Torches have been lit around the perimeter of the larger circle. The fire in the smaller circle looks freshly started, with a plume of thick white smoke rising from the center.

Caridad is pleased with the space, the arrangements of the torches, and the location of the central fire pit.

"The sun will touch the horizon in about thirty minutes," Caridad said. "Then we will be ready to begin."

Back inside, Caridad moves through each room, talking to the drummers and the other musicians. As she gives them final instructions, they move into the backyard. The sun is near the horizon, and the wind settles to a hint of breeze from the water. The sea is glistening with the reflection of sunlight.

Julian watches the musicians gathering, and the realization of what's about to happen washes over him. He returns to the house, and Caridad takes him to a small sitting room beside the kitchen. He sits on a sofa covered in dark green velvety fabric.

It's ancient but soft and comfortable. She hands him a glass of dark rum, and he sips it slowly.

"You can light the cigar now," Caridad says, smiling.

"I will need a lighter and a cutter," Julian says.

Caridad leaves Julian alone, listening to the drums and thinking about the evening ahead. A painting of a young woman in her early or mid-teens is on the opposite wall. He suspects it was commissioned to celebrate her fifteenth year. She is standing beside a chair, wearing a powder blue dress that reaches the floor, and her arm is draped casually over the back. The image combines the Indigenous, African, and Catholic religions. She is holding a small ceramic statue. A delicate gold crucifix on a gold chain hangs around her neck, completing her outfit, and her expression suggests pride and contentment.

"I understand you are looking for a lighter and cutter," Alex says, smiling as he walks into the room.

"Yes, and I'm glad you're delivering them," Julian says as he lights his cigar.

"I think I'll join you," Alex says, unwrapping and lighting a cigar he took from his pocket. He wants to say more. He wants to take one more chance at talking Julian out of what he's about to attempt, but he knows any further discussions about his misgivings would be useless.

Alex takes a draw on his cigar and exhales slowly, watching the smoke rise toward the ceiling.

"Do you expect to see your father tonight?" he asks.

"I don't know. I hope so. I don't have any specific expectations other than wanting to find closure."

"I understand," Alex says. "When I feel my grandmother in this house, it's comforting to know she is here."

"I know," Julian says. "But you express doubt about what we are doing. Beliefs are complicated, aren't they? To be Cuban is to struggle with this internal debate, the constant clash of Christian, Indigenous, and African beliefs."

"We can't sort these things out," Alex says. "We have to find our common ground, our equilibrium."

"That is true," Julian says. "The other night, when you opened the bottle of rum, you sprinkled the first sip onto the floor. We both know who that was for."

"You have me on that one, Amigo," Alex says, smiling. "But when does a superstition become a belief?"

"When you no longer think of it as a superstition," Julian says. "We cling to the old stories of creation. Why do you think that is?"

"That's easy," Alex says. "Most of us feel there has to be more to life, to our existence."

"Precisely," Julian says. "We all want there to be more to it."

Julian looked at the painting of the young girl.

"Who is she?" He asks.

"The doctor's mother when she was young," Alex says. "It was commissioned for her Quinceañera."

"It's a study in syncretization," Julian says. "She exists in three spiritual worlds. The iconography in the painting says it all: a mix of Catholic, African, and Taíno. It must mean something that the *Areyto*, a Taíno contribution to the religion practiced here, has survived hundreds of years. Given all the fantastic stories in all the religions on earth, is it hard to believe this one? What if our ancestors knew how to visit the other side? What if they did speak to those on the other side?"

"I don't know," Alex says. "This is the ceremony you and Caridad are attempting to perform."

"Yes," Julian says.

"It's a lot to take in," Alex says. "We all have stories about relatives and their religious practices. Even now, there are altars in almost every house in Cuba."

"There doesn't have to be a specific ceremony or ritual," Julian says. "Look at what you experience in this house. Your work is informed by the presence of your grandmother. There is no equivocation on your part about how real that is for you."

Caridad walks into the room, looking annoyed.

"Why is there so much talking in here?" she asks. "And so much smoke!"

Julian and Alex looked like two boys caught doing something they shouldn't.

"Alex, you come with me," Caridad says.

Julian is alone on the couch, still smoking the cigar. As he exhales, the smoke lifts into the chandelier, creating a haze in the lights. He glances up, and the smoke slowly coalesces into a scene of women dancing. This is going to be an interesting night, he thinks, as he sits and anticipates his future.

Areyto

Sitting in the room in the front of the house, Maricel watches the smoke rise slowly from the English bone china taurine in the middle of the table. She feels the effects of the cohoba powder laced into the tobacco leaves as Caridad encourages her to breathe in deeply. As she inhales, Maricel looks at the cowrie shells and polished stones on her body. Her grandmother and the other women of the lodge have been preparing her for the ritual dance since early morning. The shells and stones are ready to play their part in the ceremony.

She knows her grandmother and Julian are relying on her to open the door to the other side. She takes several deep breaths and focuses on the smoke. It reminds her of incense, and she thinks about the church in Regla and how the incense always makes her feel like she is in the presence of the Orishas.

"It's time," Caridad says as she leads Maricel down the hallway to the kitchen.

As they approach the backyard, the percussive rhythm of the drumming becomes more insistent. Many of the musicians playing the sacred batás are also priests, joined by other drummers playing traditional percussion instruments. They are in a "conversation" that is a complex mix of codified parts and improvised passages.

Maricel feels the energy from the drums as they lay down the rhythm. The dance is complex, with many complicated and strenuous moves, so she instinctively performs it in her head, reacting to the subtle changes in cadence and intensity.

The music reflects the syncretic combination of the sacred Taíno ceremony, combined with the European colonizers' Catholicism and the religious beliefs of slaves called *Lucumi*, a term used in Cuba for the African people belonging to the ethnic-linguistic group of the Yoruba. The continuous changes in tempo are producing a dense, intricate polyrhythmic texture.

Maricel glances again at the backyard. Still feeling anxious, she hopes the cohoba powder will make her relaxed and confident.

After a few minutes and with encouragement from her grandmother, Maricel walks slowly out the back door. Still apprehensive, she also feels powerful as she descends the stairs.

Approaching the stones that define the outer circle, Maricel senses the history of the space. She can feel the energy of the ceremonies performed by the Taíno long before Western Europeans arrived on the island.

Walking slowly around the circle's perimeter, she looks at each priest with an unspoken plea to send her to the spirit world. As she circles, one by one, the priest-musicians return her gaze with a respectful deference. Each nods, acknowledging her power and importance to the ceremony they are about to perform. She takes one last look at her grandmother, the High Priestess, dressed in white. Around her neck, Caridad wears the small vert-de-gris ring, the last in her possession.

Moving to the center of the circle, Maricel is dancing in sync with the bom-bom-bom, bom-bom of the batás, and the shick, shick-a-shick of the maracas and claves. She feels the music pulsing through her. The sounds and rhythms of the instruments are just as intoxicating as the cohoba powder. The Zemi images, tattooed on her body, take on a new and sacred meaning with the addition of the cowrie shells and stones. As she moves, the shells start their soft trilling, and Maricel knows the sound of the shells will pierce the veil separating her from the other side.

Louder and faster, the drums and maracas keep up the beat, and the circle begins to pulse. The music and rhythm are starting to feel different, lifting her spirit. The energy of the music and the sacred space are converging, and her dancing has merged with the music. She anticipates the undulation of the drums as they shift in tempo and intensity.

Julian

Caridad clutches her vert-de-gris ring as she leads Julian into the circle's center and instructs him to sit next to the ancient fire pit. She faces him east, toward Baracoa and Yuké. Maricel can see he looks nervous as her grandmother gives him final instructions.

Caridad hopes Julian will contact his father, but her main motivation is to allow the spirits to inform him of his true destiny. It has been so many years since her grandfather's death, and she fears it has taken her too long to find a successor. When the dream about Julian started, she didn't think it had anything to do with her search. But after meeting Phoebe and Mera on the plane, she knows it is all connected. The rings kept the connection, and Phoebe and Mera led her to Julian through them.

"Close your eyes," was the last thing she said to Julian as she walked out of the circle, but they weren't the last words she spoke. Halfway between Julian and the perimeter of the circle of priests, Caridad spoke the words entrusted to her by her grandfather. They were the words first spoken by the Taíno Caciques, who heard them from the Zemi spirits. It had been a long time since they were spoken out loud and even longer since they were spoken as part of the sacred *Areyto* ceremony. She had no idea how many others knew the secret incantation, and she didn't know who she would trust with it before she no longer remembered it. She hopes it's Julian but knows that decision isn't hers.

Julian watches Maricel as she walks around the circle, hypnotized by her movement and excited about what her dancing will set in motion. With one last look at Caridad, he closes his eyes and waits.

Bom-bom-bom, bom-bom, shick, shick-a-shick . . .

Maricel's dancing intensifies, and while preserving the traditional style, she is adapting the ancient choreography to her interpretation.

Bom-bom-bom, bom-bom, shick, shick-a-shick . . .

Julian feels the vibration and energy created by the music and Maricel's dancing coming up through him from the ground.

With a shiver, Maricel lifts her head slowly, looking at the light that is no longer the moon but the doorway to the other side. She has found the path to the other side, and the spirits and ancestors are calling.

Sensing danger, Maricel wonders if something is wrong. Either way, she knows she has to continue to dance, strengthening her connection to the music. The closer she gets to the rhythm, the more energy she feels. She is slipping into the spirit world, and the reality of what is about to happen washes over her.

In the
Name of the Father

In Baracoa, Yuké stirs beneath a light mist, breaking its long silence with a gentle rumble, a vibration resonating as the energy of the island's east side asserts itself. Julian is sitting on the ground next to the fire. The drumming echoes loudly. The trilling of Maricel's shells and bracelets sounds like the flutter of wings, and Julian sees a black witch moth. He knows the moth is a sign, and his decision to accept it has brought him to this moment.

With his eyes closed but seeing with perfect clarity, it has come to this: the sea, the smoke, the music, and the dancing. Julian feels his life is folding in on itself, and images flash: On the Malecón with Max, where three, white-crowned pigeons take flight. In Old Havana, with Ileana, she pleads with him not to leave. Then, a leap to Key West boulevard, with a vision of Havana suspended in mid-air. The Prado and Malecón seem to exist in two places simultaneously. Finally, he eats freshly caught shark at the Finca with his father and toasts Ernest Hemingway on his birth and death anniversary.

The Cohoba powder and the dancing are having their intended effect—his attention shifts to the fire—the smoke ascending into the sky unaffected by the gentle breeze. Through the lingering haze, and in his mind's eye, the flat top of Yuké materializes, rising like an apparition. Maricel's dancing and the music create a wave that lifts him out of Mariel into the mountain in Baracoa, where he feels his soul settle into the sacred space.

Bom-bom-bom, bom-bom, shick, shick-a-shick . . .

Maricel moves past him, and as she does, Julian sees someone moving toward him. The familiar figure is dressed in shorts and a plain collared shirt, and he knows it's his father.

Ramón is standing next to a stone altar illuminated with hundreds of candles. He is in his mid-forties, looking fit and content. He is holding a machete in his right hand.

"I miss you, old man," Julian says.

"We will be together soon enough," Ramón says.

Julian sees the machete, which reminds him of Ramón's sacrifices: two years of work in the sugar cane fields, work he had never done.

"Those two years you spent in the fields. It was all new to you but you learned and survived," Julian said to his father. "Your machete, you called *La Mocha*, the Blade. You always said it looked like a shark cutting down the sugar cane. Faster and faster, you worked, and no man could put you to shame. You are a descendant of Taíno, Congolese, and Spanish. You had Mambí blood and courage in your veins. You were of flesh and bone, but as much as they tried, they couldn't break you. They couldn't because of your love for your family. You chopped for long hours under the relentless Cuban sun, and the stalks slashed your skin. You consecrated the land with your blood and earned freedom for yourself and your family."

Ramón holds out his arms, and Julian sees the scars from the sugar cane.

"*La Mocha*," Ramón says, smiling and remembering. "The Blade! These scars mean everything to me. There was only one way out, and I took it. I have no regrets, not even in this place. I miss you, my son. But you know what you have to do."

"I wish that were true," Julian says. "You taught me so much. But I wasn't ready to be on my own. Now I am struggling to find my way."

"There is never enough time in a life to accomplish all you want," Ramón says. "There are always regrets. I cheated death a couple of times because I learned a few tricks along the way. Like old boxers, I did just enough to avoid being knocked out. Death lets us cheat to lull us into complacency. It waits patiently for our arrogance to betray us. With age comes wisdom, but unfortunately, death is always wiser. You will learn this soon enough. The people who see death coming are the lucky ones. They have time to say goodbye to those they love. For the rest of us, those whom death chooses to snatch in the blink of an eye, the journey to the other side can be blissful or painful, depending on the circumstances. Be ready, my son, your time will come, and you will know what you must do."

Ramón turned and walked back toward the altar, disappearing into the smoke from the candles.

Julian follows him with his eyes, and the sadness grips him as his father slowly disappears.

The drums, maracas, and claves are more urgent than ever.

Bom-bom-bom, bom-bom, shick, shick-a-shick . . .

Julian opens his eyes, and he is no longer inside Yuké. Maricel collapses, and Caridad rushes to her.

The drumming stops suddenly, and the silence is as jolting as the music had been a second before.

Several drummers rush over to Maricel, and Alex comes to Julian.

"Are you OK?" Alex asked. "What happened?"

Julian is weak and dizzy.

"I don't know," Julian says. "I'm having trouble remembering."

The combination of the rum, cigar, and cohoba powder has given him a wicked headache.

"I need to lie down," he says.

Alex helps Julian up and walks him to the house.

"I have a place for you," Alex says. "It's upstairs. Do you think you can make it?"

"Yes, I can make it."

Alex takes Julian upstairs to the bedroom at the back of the house. From the window, Julian sees the fire pit and the smoke rising with his father's spirit. He hears his father's voice—"You know what you have to do."

Returning downstairs, Alex sees Caridad and Maricel in the hallway. Maricel looks exhausted.

"She needs to rest," Caridad says.

Alex finds a place for Maricel to rest and goes back upstairs. Finding Julian asleep, he leaves a note explaining his plan to return in the morning.

Alex packs up his belongings and heads back to Havana.

That was six hours ago, and the house has been silent. Silent but not dark. Alex left the chandeliers lit so Julian would not be confused if he woke up during the night. Each room is bathed in the soft glow of the light, with the cut crystals glinting slightly and looking suspended in the air.

By the Light

All houses wherein men have lived and died
Are haunted houses. Through the open doors
The harmless phantoms on their errands glide,
With feet that make no sound upon the floors.

— *Henry Wadsworth Longfellow*

It's three o'clock, and the moon is at its zenith. The sea has calmed, and the birds are asleep, except for the nighthawks, patrolling the mangroves and fruit trees, looking for their dinner.

Angelita knows she followed the young dancer on her return from the other side, but how she managed to do that is a mystery to her. Even though she feels out of place and at the wrong time, she knows exactly what she is supposed to do. She must find the priest. His name is Julian, and he is being summoned, as she was, so many years ago.

It has been a long time since the doctor's house was aglow in the middle of the night. The chandeliers were always Angelita's favorite part of the house. Being lit into the wee hours of the morning meant a great gathering had taken place, and the conversation had lasted well past its official end.

At the end of a long evening, the doctor and his wife would ascend the stairs, check on the children, and retire to their bedroom at the back of the house.

"Leave it, Angelita," the doctor would say. "We will clean it up in the morning."

But Angelita would not leave it. She loved the ritual of closing each room, turning off the lights, and straightening up as needed. She would move through each room slowly and quietly to avoid disturbing those sleeping upstairs. Every room had its stories and memories, and Angelita loved reliving all of them. Moving through the house at night in the quiet with everyone else asleep gave her a sense of home.

On this night, after so many years of being away, Angelita, summoned from the other side by Maricel and the musicians, is praying in a whisper. She has performed her ritual downstairs, except she could not turn off the chandeliers. Now, she has ascended the stairs and is moving toward the real reason for her presence.

Julian is asleep in what used to be the doctor's bedroom—a room intimately familiar to her. Standing in the doorway, she looks out through the large window onto the upstairs porch, past the railing, and down to the long, sweeping lawn. The fire is still smoldering, and a thin trail of smoke is rising.

Julian is visible in the moon's faint light, still holding its own in the clear night sky. He is sound asleep, and she stops momentarily to listen to his slow, steady breathing.

"Wake up, Maestro," she says in her low, thin, whisper voice. "Wake up."

To Julian, her voice sounds like palm fronds rustling in the breeze. After a moment, he rolls over and looks out the window. As he begins to stir, he isn't sure where he is.

Angelita calls to him again. "Wake up, fine priest."

Julian is awake at the sound of the mystery voice.

"Come with me, Maestro," Angelita says.

He sits up and looks toward the doorway and the stairs. The house is quiet but not dark, as the light from the chandeliers downstairs creates a soft amber glow.

"Come with me, Maestro," Angelita repeats. "We must go."

The voice sounded strange, and Julian didn't recognize it, but somehow, he knew it was Angelita. He was looking for something and hesitated to rise and follow her. He knew he was going, but he must do something first.

"Downstairs," Angelita says in her thin, palm-frond voice, her only voice now.

When he is done, Julian stands, still dressed in the clothes he was wearing when he arrived at the house and makes his way to the stairs. The hallway is filled with amber light, brighter at the bottom but not too bright, soft, and welcoming. He descends slowly, going to the hallway on the first floor.

"This way," Angelita whispers.

Julian follows her voice. He turns and walks to the back of the house, through the kitchen, and out the back door. He is standing in the yard looking at the small tendril of smoke rising out of the fire pit. He remembers seeing his father rising out of the fire as the memory of the evening comes back to him.

"You know what you have to do," his father says.

The encounter with Ramón left Julian with more questions than answers. Ramón looked at peace, but Julian still didn't know where he was. There was no indication that Ramón had crossed safely to the other side.

Angelita whispers, "Come with me," as she moves toward the shore.

Julian follows Angelita's voice toward the water, his father's words fresh in his mind.

At the water's edge, he looks north to the horizon and sees a soft glow, barely perceptible but real.

"Go," Angelita says.

Julian enters the water. The sand is firm, and the water feels cool.

"You know what you have to do."

Julian stands momentarily at the water's edge, and his father's meaning finally becomes clear. *His father said you know what you must do*, and now he does know—he must swim.

The motion of his arms in the water reminds him of his father in the sugar cane fields.

La Mocha! The Blade!

Julian imagines his father cutting down the sugar cane. Ramón moves through the field with relentless energy, leaving a wide open space in his path as he moves toward Julian, coming steadily closer.

The faint light in the distance is brighter now, sweeping the horizon in a slow motion like a searchlight or a lighthouse.

Ninety miles away, the Sand Key Lighthouse sits on a sand bar off Key West. It swings its beam around and points it at Mariel. "There's no way," Julian remembers Max saying.

"I have to tell Max," Julian says aloud, even though he knows no one can hear him.

Waist deep in the water, Julian starts swimming toward the light. It's a long way off, but it doesn't matter. The distance doesn't matter. When he reaches the light, he will tell Max, and then Max will understand. The world will be back to its natural state. His world will be back, and Max will realize what he has been trying to say for all these months: the closeness, the sameness, the connection.

La Mocha. Closer now, ever closer.

Julian is swimming, concentrating on the light.

The machete, *La Mocha*, the Blade, swings toward him. The movement is swift as the blade arcs toward his shoulders.

At the last moment, Julian sees the reflection of moonlight on the steel. Or is it the arcing light from the lighthouse ninety miles away?

And then . . .

Darkness.

Julian has stopped swimming.

There is only darkness—silence and darkness. Julian recalls his father's earlier instruction; "Remember the darkness."

"Remember the darkness." Julian hears his father speaking to him. It's as if Ramón is standing next to him. "Remember the darkness . . ."

Julian never saw the bull shark.

To him, it is the machete, *La Mocha*, the sleek and sharp blade wielded by someone who is an expert.

Someone like his father.

La Mocha!

Darkness. Then Silence. Then Calm . . .

The transition is easy. Julian realizes at the last moment that he has been preparing for it for most of his life: a small but significant shift in the light and shadows, barely perceptible to anyone but him. His arms are no longer moving. He is gliding through the water into another place.

The Sand Key light makes one more pass, arcing across the distance. It's stronger now, closer, much closer.

Angelita is gone. Caridad and Maricel are gone. His father and mother are gone. Phoebe and Mera are gone. Ileana is gone.

He left the notes and the ring as markers, but the trail will be hard to follow. There will be no reunions, no reconciliations, at least not soon.

Getting used to his new surroundings will take time, but he knows the journey will be glorious. *There is much work to do*, he thinks to himself. *I have to find Max. I have to tell Max.*

Tíaquena

Caridad was sitting in her parlor in Guanabacoa under the watchful eyes of the Virgin of Regla when she was jolted awake by a shift in the island's energy. Having given away all but the last ring, she had never felt so sure about a gift and had never been so excited about the future.

There had been many changes in her life. Sometimes, she thought it doesn't pay to live too long—the curse of knowing and seeing too much.

Maricel is asleep in her bedroom, and Caridad can hear her thrashing. On the way back from Mariel, she relayed the message a young girl had delivered during her visit to the other side. It wasn't a message for Julian; it was a message for Caridad. The young girl, who said her name was Tíaquena, had danced the night the Europeans arrived in Baracoa. It was the last night her people would live in peace. Once the invaders landed, the Taíno would face unimaginable torment, death, and destruction. But that was a long time ago. The young girl's message to Caridad was that she, Caridad, and Maricel were the future. Connected by blood over the centuries and by the unbroken chain of chiefs that had survived and endured miraculously without being discovered and killed, the legacy of her people belonged to them.

Caridad had done what she had been asked—she had found the priest and sent Julian on his journey—but her work was not done. She and Maricel had not fulfilled their destiny.

As she contemplated the days ahead, she lit a candle on the altar covered with the embroidered cloth her grandmother had given her, and gently touched the three stones in the center of the vessel that made up the focal point of her connection to the ancestors and the Orishas. She was happy to know she was still needed. She rose slowly from her chair at the front of the house and moved to the bedroom.

She knew she would sleep well, and that morning would mean the start of her new adventure.

Alex

Alex had not slept. On the drive home to Havana after the ceremony, he couldn't shake the feeling that he made a mistake leaving Julian alone in the house in Mariel. Now, he was desperate to return and find his friend safe and ready to move on from the previous night's adventure. It was early, but Alex knew he would feel much better once he saw Julian.

He pulled into the yard and found what he expected at such an early hour: silence and emptiness. Even the chickens were taking the morning off. The sun was starting to rise over the mangroves and small houses to the east. The sea was calm, and it was impossible to see if the Gulf Stream was running close or offshore.

Alex opened the front door and walked inside. The chandeliers were still lit, as he expected, and the house was quiet. He walked slowly and quietly to the back of the house. As he made his way, the only sound was the slight creaking of the pine flooring as it relented ever so slightly under his weight.

No one was in the back of the house, but the door was open. Given the previous night's activities, Alex thought this was curious but not alarming.

He walked to the open door and looked out toward the shoreline. There was a vague sense of a presence as he looked out toward the ocean, but he ignored it as another sign of his fatigue and apprehension.

Walking back toward the front of the house and up the stairs, he expected Julian to still be sound asleep in the back bedroom, where he had left him only a few hours ago.

Alex would reflect on his premonition in the coming weeks. He would remember the nagging feeling that things were not okay—the feeling his mind chose to ignore. But in the few moments before he looked into the bedroom, he was not paying attention to any of those feelings. He was not listening to his heart as it tried to tell him his friend was gone.

Alex stood frozen in the doorway, trying to process what he was seeing—or, more correctly, what he wasn't seeing—Julian wasn't there. Maybe he had gotten up and moved into another room, Alex thought. The problem was that there was no place to sleep in any other bedrooms, having all been converted into workrooms.

Alex checked the bathroom, but no Julian. He stood for a long time staring into the empty bathroom before returning to the room where he last saw his friend.

He walked over to the nightstand. What was he going to tell Delia? What was he going to tell Max, Mera, and Phoebe? Maybe he took a walk, Alex thought. Perhaps he got restless and decided to explore down by the water. Trying not to panic, Alex spotted a small round item on the nightstand on the other side of the bed. He walked over and found a small vert-de-gris ring resting on a small piece of paper. The ring was about an inch and a half in diameter and about a half-inch thick. It was old.

There were two pieces of paper. One was rolled up and pushed inside the ring. Alex pulled it out and unrolled it. He recognized Julian's handwriting:

For Ileana . . . I will find you.

He moved the ring aside, and the second piece of paper was flat on the table. In Julian's small, neat handwriting were the words:

Please tell Max I have gone ahead.

When he read the instructions and message, Alex knew it would be a long time before he saw his friend again.

October Moon

—————•··•·••·—————

Ileana

"No one you love is ever truly lost."

— *Ernest Hemingway*

The violin music was barely audible on the street in Old Havana as it lifted onto the moist air, which had the coolness of an October breeze.

Ileana was up early, as she was every morning, and the music she was playing had taken on a sadness that only she and her closest friends could discern. She remembered the last morning she spent with Julian; it was both a comfort and a curse. She wouldn't trade it for anything, but the swiftness with which it had happened and the sense of loss from knowing what her world could have been was a torment that even her music could not ease.

The melody unfolds—a lament of lost love and lost dreams. Ileana's fingers are on the fingerboard, tracing its contours and defining the melody. Her eyes, half-closed, peering into a realm where time bends, and loneliness knows no bounds. The violin has become a vessel—an ark for Ileana's grief.

She glances over at the small ring on the table next to her and the note Julian had written, and she could perceive his presence. But she could no longer see or touch him. She remembered Julian expressing frustration about being unable to communicate with his father. It was his desire to communicate that had sent him on his journey. Now she understood, so she awoke every morning and played, hoping the sound of her violin would bring him to her.

I am here her violin said, with the pleading sounds of the song Julian had heard in Baracoa as a young boy.

Please find me.

Mera

Mera wakes to the sounds of drums and clavés, except she isn't in Havana; she's home, and the drums and claves are her alarm playing a cruel trick. After her initial disappointment, she rolls over, turns the alarm off, and reaches for the ring. She always sleeps with the ring, afraid the dream won't come if she doesn't. It doesn't always come, but it comes if she's patient and doesn't think too hard about it. She can't imagine it not coming. It sustains her. She wonders if it sustains him. It's always the same, but sometimes, in the dream, she's confused if they're in Paris or Havana. Even though she knows they are in Paris, she likes it when her mind confuses her. Dreams are so strange. Hers is lovely and sweet, even though it ends sadly.

It's still dark outside, and the windows are wet with the thick, humid blanket of a Florida fog so prevalent in October. As always, she will do her usual chores this morning and get ready for work. But it's not the same today. Max is in Key West, Phoebe has left for California, and Julian hasn't been heard from since he disappeared in Havana. While her life is made up of so much more than her connection with her friends, being so far from all of them has left her with a deep sense of loneliness. She will text later and check in, but it won't be the same.

As she moves to the bathroom, she notices the small painting Julian gave her before they left for Havana for the last time. It's the painting of the three sisters. He told her the one in the middle was her. She knew this wasn't true because it had been painted several years before they met, but Julian always had a way of saying things that made them seem true, even if they weren't. He told her this the night they all had dinner at Alex's. It was the last time they would be together and truly and honestly happy. It wasn't uncomplicated. It was complicated between the four of them, but always authentic and honest, and that rarely happened in real life.

After Julian disappeared, she realized that a part of her stayed in Havana, and a part remained in Paris. She wondered if someone's soul could be divided into pieces to exist in moments so meaningful there wasn't any way to leave them entirely. Was a tiny part of her still sitting at the café in Paris? Was a part of her still sitting in the lobby of the Ambos Mundos Hotel in Old Havana? She was imagining the old man playing the piano. It, too, was a part of her, the sound of that piano and the scent of the lobby, caught in the 1950s.

She stared at the painting for a few more minutes. The woman in the middle was smiling at her. *She looks happy,* Mera thought. *She will always look happy.*

She went back to the bed and picked up her phone. The hell with texting, she thought. It was early, but she needed to hear Max's voice. She needed a connection to that world, to Paris and Havana.

The phone started to ring, and she was already feeling better.

Maximillian

I am standing at the eastern end of Smather's Beach in Key West, staring south toward Havana. It's late afternoon, and people are walking and biking on the broad sidewalk that separates the beach from the road. Three months ago, I dreamt I was standing on the Malecón with Julian, looking north and imagining this spot. For the last two months, I've had an unshakeable desire to see the Gulf Stream from the Key West side.

I imagine seeing people strolling the Prado in 1934 from where I'm standing. I imagine Julian walking with them. No one in Key West has seen Havana in the mist since that night; at least, no one would admit it. Does it manifest itself every night? Did we become too cynical to see it? Maybe it became too disappointed in us to show itself. Or the people of Havana and Key West no longer connect spiritually. Sixty years of separation has made the ninety miles of Gulf Stream broader and deeper than it was in 1934.

The sun is hugging the horizon, promising another famous Key West sunset. I remember the evening three months ago on the Malecón as if it happened. I remember the buildings and the light reflecting off the new windows and paint. I remember the young lovers and the fishermen along the wall. The fishermen were annoyed at the waves, and the young lovers embraced them as if the spray were a baptism of their love for each other.

Havana is so close—ninety miles.

"On a hazy afternoon in 1934, there was a Vision as the sun was setting."

Light and shadows playing tricks across the Gulf Stream.

I take several deep breaths, and the people moving along the sidewalk start to fade. As the sun moves closer to the horizon and the shadows grow longer, a line of low, thin clouds appears to the south. The sun touches the horizon, and I hear Julian's voice. He's reading from the yellowed clipping:

"Shortly after 6 o'clock last Friday, there gradually appeared a peculiar looking haze apparently about three miles above the horizon and just as though it was a moving picture where the spirit like a semblance of a scene or persons gradually appears . . ."

"Seeing across is a myth," I told him, and I remember his disappointment. I wish I hadn't said it. I wish it weren't true.

Julian

When I returned home from Key West, the dreams started again. I wrote them down as they came to me in the same journal I used when we visited Finca Vigía and Julian's Aunt Nita's house after the first Colloquium. As it was back then, I could only begin my day once I filled in the blanks and added new details. There are people in this story who are real, and some who are imagined. As I was describing them and the role they played, the real and the imagined blended. I never tried to separate them. I don't think it matters.

The dreams have faded over the past few years, but I still imagine Julian disappearing in a haze of sacred rhythms and ancient chants—transported by the Orishas, his ancestors, and the Gulf Stream to the "other side," the afterlife. I imagine him in the house in Mariel, surrounded by the chandeliers, deciding to make his final journey from this life to the next. Summoned by his father and accompanied by Angelita, he would know he was doing the right thing. He would know he was fulfilling his destiny.

It's not hard for me to imagine these things, but the truth is that Julian never answered the wake-up call I made to him the morning we were supposed to leave for Havana. I was concerned when he didn't answer, so I called a neighbor, a friend of his, to check on him. The neighbor found him in his studio, collapsed in front of a painting of two fishermen carrying their catch on a stick. Julian had died suddenly the night before of a heart attack. When the neighbor called to give me the bad news, for some reason he mentioned the fishermen in the painting. He said they looked tired. I think Julian was tired, too.

EPILOGUE

The dreams tell Julian's story, a story he never lived, at least not in this life. Now, in the space between the light and the shadows, between sleep and awake, I see him strolling across the Plaza de Armas in Old Havana, down Obispo Street. Dressed in a white *guayabera,* the people he passes take note of him as he walks proudly with confidence and purpose. The pace of the city transitions from daytime to nighttime, and the Ambos Mundos begins its chameleon transformation from pink to rose to deep rust. Rain has fallen, and the old city surrenders the day's heat. The dust has settled, and the light transitions from daylight to warm amber, reflecting the afterglow of the day's energy.

Once inside the Ambos Mundos, with the ghost of Hemingway as his companion, Julian sits at the bar, chatting with the bartender and drinking an ice-cold Bucanero. An old man is playing the ancient piano in the lobby, and Julian walks over and places a ten-dollar Cuban convertible peso bill in the tip jar. The music transports the lobby to Havana in the 1950s or Paris in the 1930s—the lost generation found.

I am comforted by this last dream and grateful it still comes to me. It means a part of Julian lives on. It's a reminder that the people whose lives he touched with his kindness and his art are better for having known him.

Some souls vibrate on a higher frequency; Julian was one of those souls.

~ End ~

www.ingramcontent.com/pod-product-compliance
Lightning Source LLC
Chambersburg PA
CBHW051148030726
47504CB00004B/1091